Sweet Surrender

Also by Liliana Hart

THE MACKENZIE SERIES

Dane
A Christmas Wish: Dane
Thomas
To Catch A Cupid: Thomas
Riley
Fireworks: Riley
Cooper
A MacKenzie Christmas
MacKenzie Box Set
Cade
Shadows and Silk
Secrets and Satin
Sins and Scarlet Lace
The MacKenzie Security Series *(Includes the 3 books listed above)*
1001 Dark Nights: Captured in Surrender
Sizzle
Crave
Troublemaker
Scorch
Spies and Stilettos

THE COLLECTIVE SERIES

Kill Shot

THE RENA DRAKE SERIES

Breath of Fire

ADDISON HOLMES MYSTERIES

Whiskey Rebellion
Whiskey Sour
Whiskey For Breakfast

Whiskey, You're The Devil
Whiskey Tango Foxtrot

JJ GRAVES MYSTERIES

Dirty Little Secrets
A Dirty Shame
Dirty Rotten Scoundrel
Down and Dirty
Dirty Deeds

STANDALONE NOVELS/NOVELLAS

All About Eve
Paradise Disguised
Catch Me If You Can

Sweet Surrender

A MacKenzie Family Novella

By Liliana Hart

1001 Dark Nights

Sweet Surrender
A MacKenzie Family Novella
By Liliana Hart

1001 Dark Nights

ISBN: 978-1-942299-41-7

Published by Evil Eye Concepts, Incorporated

Dedication

To Scott~

Because we get to do life together. And we're a heck of a team. Thank you always for your unwavering support and love.

Acknowledgments from the Author

A huge thank you to MJ Rose and Liz Berry at Evil Eye Publishing for being the most awesome publishers ever, Jillian Stein for being a social media genius, and all the other 1001 Dark Nights authors who make this so much fun.

Sign up for the 1001 Dark Nights Newsletter
and be entered to win a Tiffany Key necklace.

There's a contest every month!

Go to www.1001DarkNights.com to subscribe.

As a bonus, all subscribers will receive a free
1001 Dark Nights story
The First Night
by Lexi Blake & M.J. Rose

One Thousand and One Dark Nights

Once upon a time, in the future…

I was a student fascinated with stories and learning. I studied philosophy, poetry, history, the occult, and the art and science of love and magic. I had a vast library at my father's home and collected thousands of volumes of fantastic tales.

I learned all about ancient races and bygone times. About myths and legends and dreams of all people through the millennium. And the more I read the stronger my imagination grew until I discovered that I was able to travel into the stories... to actually become part of them.

I wish I could say that I listened to my teacher and respected my gift, as I ought to have. If I had, I would not be telling you this tale now.
But I was foolhardy and confused, showing off with bravery.

One afternoon, curious about the myth of the Arabian Nights, I traveled back to ancient Persia to see for myself if it was true that every day Shahryar (Persian: شهريار*, "king") married a new virgin, and then sent yesterday's wife to be beheaded. It was written and I had read, that by the time he met Scheherazade, the vizier's daughter, he'd killed one thousand women.*

Something went wrong with my efforts. I arrived in the midst of the story and somehow exchanged places with Scheherazade – a phenomena that had never occurred before and that still to this day, I cannot explain.

Now I am trapped in that ancient past. I have taken on Scheherazade's life and the only way I can protect myself and stay alive is to do what she did to protect herself and stay alive.

Every night the King calls for me and listens as I spin tales. And when the evening ends and dawn breaks, I stop at a point that leaves him breathless and yearning for more. And so the King spares my life for one more day, so that he might hear the rest of my dark tale.

As soon as I finish a story... I begin a new one... like the one that you, dear reader, have before you now.

Chapter One

A brisk March wind blew through Surrender.

"Being a cop doesn't mean I crave donuts." Grant Boone glared out the window toward the bakery across the street.

Cooper MacKenzie snorted, "You *were* a cop."

Grant's hands fisted in his lap and his gaze dropped to stare at them as the familiar anger raged through his body. His light brown hair, which was long overdue for a cut, hung down to hide his expression. He knew Cooper hadn't meant anything by it, but *damn*, the words still pierced him like a knife to the gut.

"My mistake," he said. "I *was* a cop."

"Come on, Grant. You know I didn't mean it that way. Hell, you're still the best there is. Your chief will wake up and realize his screw-up before long. Though I've always thought you and the city would clash before too long. Hell, look at you. You look like you walked out of one of those *Marlboro* commercials. What the hell is a country boy like you doing in Detroit anyway?"

Cooper wasn't the first person to tell him he didn't belong in the Motor City. But he'd served the city with a purpose. He'd worked undercover, and he'd been an asset to the force. It wasn't often they came across a six-foot-five, two-hundred-and-forty-five pound bruiser to work the biker bars and clubs.

"There's no going back, Coop. I gave that shithole city the best years of my life. And for what? A forced retirement under a cloud of an internal affairs investigation." Grant set his coffee on the desk and knuckled his eyes. He couldn't remember the last time he'd slept a full night through. God, was he tired.

A bright red BMW SUV sped down Main Street, kicking up leaves as it turned with a squeal of tires and parked illegally at the side of the little bakery across the street.

"Holy shit," Grant said, bringing his boots down to the floor with a thump. "Who is that maniac?"

"Damn," Cooper said, whistling through his teeth. "I'm going to have to give her a ticket this time. We've warned her about the speed three times already. But you're going to want to steer clear of that mess." Cooper brought his own feet down and pushed back his chair. "She's nothing but trouble."

Grant forgot his own problems back in Detroit as he watched the woman with fascination. The driver's side door opened, and a pair of fancy cowboy boots touched the cobbled street. By the time she stood to her full height his mouth was already watering. Pure lust rolled deep in his belly. She looked like a modern-day Xena Warrior Princess with black hair and the body of an Amazon. He couldn't see her eye color from that distance, but in his mind they had to be blue.

She unloaded a large stack of white boxes from the back of the Beemer, and he watched her mouth move in what could only be curses as she fought to keep hold of them in the wind.

He could tell by looking the woman was an absolute hellcat. He'd tussled with them before, and he had a knack for attracting them. He'd worked most of his career undercover, but he always seemed to connect with dangerous women who added an extra element of risk to his drug enforcement days.

Grant grinned and shook his head. "Damn, Coop. You shouldn't have said that. You know I love a good warning."

"Her name's Liza Carmichael," Cooper said. "Her great aunt

passed not long ago. She ran that bakery for fifty years. Mrs. Baker never missed a morning's opening. Though I seem to recall her coming in late once after she buried her husband in the early nineties."

"The old lady who owned the bakery was named Mrs. Baker?" Grant asked.

"Ironic, huh?"

"So Surrender has a new pastry chef," Grant said. "Maybe I'll take up donut eating after all. Once a cop, always a cop."

Cooper laughed and shook his head. "You always were a glutton for punishment."

"I miss the adrenaline rush."

"Hey, I know what you mean. And I'm not saying you should swear off donuts, but honestly, I'd stay away from her. She's made it crystal clear that her intentions are to lease the space or sell it outright. Whichever brings her the greatest profit. She has no desire to stay in Surrender."

"Perfect," he said. "Neither do I."

Grant ran his fingers through his hair, pushing it back off his face, and he noticed Cooper's scowl as his gaze locked on the disfiguring scar that ran the length of his left jaw to just behind his ear. He knew Cooper still carried the guilt of the injury, but there was nothing he or anyone could've done. It was just an undercover drug deal gone bad.

"Coop," he said, trying to divert attention back to the very sexy Ms. Carmichael. "I can assure you that I will never swear off donuts. I have a powerful sweet tooth."

"Are we still talking about actual donuts?"

"There's all kinds of donuts," he said, smiling. "And I've got a hell of an appetite."

Cooper grabbed the sheriff's cowboy hat off the stand behind his desk, snugged it on his head, and grabbed his sheepskin coat.

"What the hell?" Cooper said. "Things have been slow around here lately, and I need a good laugh. She's going to tear you up, brother."

Grant slapped Cooper on the shoulder and grabbed his own coat as he followed him out of the office. "It feels just like old times."

* * * *

Liza Carmichael fumbled with another case of cake boxes. It was her eighth trip into the old building. Each time she schlepped back out to her car to get another load, and then schlepped back inside again, fighting the wind and the door, she wondered why Aunt Rose had left her the bakery. She had other family, but instead, she'd left it all to Liza.

Liza remembered visits during the summers when her folks would make the short drive down from Canada. It was Aunt Rose who'd taught her to bake, telling her stories of each of the family recipes and saying everything in her shop was made with love and great memories. And she'd nurtured Liza's natural talent in the kitchen. The summer visits had stopped after her parents had divorced, but she'd always remembered those times with Aunt Rose. Apparently, Aunt Rose had remembered them too.

The memories were distant now, and nostalgia had no place in her life. Surrender, Montana, was only a detour on her way to Los Angeles.

New York had been her home for the last two years, but after the crash, she'd decided a fresh start was in order as far away from her ex-fiancé as possible. Most of that need for a fresh start and putting three thousand miles between them had to do with the fact that she'd driven Richard's Mercedes C-class coupe right into his condo as he and his *other* girlfriend were busy breaking in the new comforter set Liza had just bought. Now that she knew that romance and happily-ever-afters were a crock of shit, it was time to focus on two things—herself and her career.

Her pointy-toed, rhinestone-studded boot kicked against the bakery door. The bell, originally hung by her great aunt and uncle, tinkled irritatingly once again. She let the empty boxes spill from her hands and join the other white pastry boxes that covered the hardwood floor.

She blew choppy bangs from her eyes and flopped into one of the wrought-iron chairs that sat around small round tables.

"This is ridiculous. You always had a hell of a sense of humor, Aunt Rose."

She rolled her shoulders and relaxed, eyeing the glass showcase filled with pastries and cakes. She'd had to close for twenty minutes after the morning rush when she'd run out of confectioner boxes.

The beautiful display stared back at her mockingly. She had the gift. Just like her great aunt. For a woman who loved physical fitness and extreme sports, it was damned inconvenient to be a cake-making maven.

"I am not getting trapped in this one-horse town," she said, almost convincing herself. "I'm selling. And that's final. Fifty years of batter and frosting is long enough. I've got a life to live, and cake making for cowboys ain't it."

She nudged the boxes with the toe of her boot and then sighed as she got out of the chair and knelt to scoop them up. When she stood back up, her gaze locked on the handsome sight walking in her direction, and her lips quirked in a smile.

Cooper MacKenzie was nothing to sneeze at, but those MacKenzie boys had been all trouble and sex appeal when she'd visited during the summers of her youth. Her great aunt had warned her often to stay away from them, and she had, for the most part, but she'd have been lying if she'd said she hadn't sneaked a peek with longing every once in a while.

But the wildness must've calmed over the years because Cooper was very happily married and proud to show it, though he was still something to look at—that thick black hair and those cobalt blue eyes—the body he obviously kept in shape and the tattoos that covered his arms.

But it was the man who walked beside him that was worth a second look in her book. He moved with an ease that told her he was very comfortable in his own skin. His shoulders were broad, and even through the layers of his work shirt and coat she could tell that he was in good shape—*excellent* shape, actually. His light brown hair was unruly and on the longish side and the scruff on his face let her know he hadn't seen a razor in a couple of days.

"Well, hello, cowboy," she purred.

And she felt the slow burn of attraction dance deep within her—a burn that she'd thought had fizzled to nonexistence since the disaster of her last relationship. It was nice to know that things were still in working order. And it was even nicer to know that maybe she could find a bit of excitement in Surrender after all.

She'd been in Surrender for a few weeks, and it had been the longest few weeks of her life. She was a city girl and had always been a city girl. What was she supposed to do when everything closed by six o'clock every evening? Except for Duffey's, which was the little bar at the very end of Main Street. But she'd learned quickly enough that there was no excitement to be had watching a bunch of men play darts and pool and tell lies.

The population was small in Surrender and it was, for the most part, a ranching community, which meant early to bed and early to rise. And she'd fallen in with the crowd because she was up baking every morning by four o'clock. She was awake before the roosters.

She hurried and tossed the boxes behind the showcase, and combed her bangs with her fingers so they hopefully looked artfully tousled instead of like she'd been hauling boxes in a windstorm.

The little bell above the door rang and the wind whirled in with them before they hurriedly shut the door.

"Damn," she muttered under her breath. He was even better looking up close and personal.

She'd said it under her breath, but by the way he smirked at her she had the feeling he knew exactly what she was thinking. She wasn't the kind of woman who liked a man to be spit shined and polished. She liked a man who knew how to work with his hands and who looked like he spent time in the sun. And if he had a little edge to him, all the better. And this guy definitely had an edge in his worn biker boots and tattered jeans.

Part of her wondered if she should just tell them she was closed, but she'd never been a coward.

"Hey, there," she said, not taking her gaze off of the stranger. "What can I do for you?"

"A loaded question, if I've ever heard one," he said.

"Oh, for the love of God," Cooper interrupted. "I want a bear claw and a fresh cup of coffee. You make it better than what I can do at the sheriff's office."

"You got it, Sheriff," she said, going to get his order. Her gaze still strayed to the stranger as she worked.

"What about you, cowboy? What do you want?"

"I'm swearing off donuts," he said in a slow drawl.

Cooper snorted out a laugh, but she ignored him.

"That's a damned shame," she said, feeling herself go hot all over. "I don't think you've ever tasted one of my donuts. They'll melt in your mouth."

Good Lord, what was she doing? She was practically seducing this man in her great aunt's bakery. She'd never be able to look Cooper MacKenzie in the eye again. But she couldn't seem to help herself. And from the heat in his dark brown eyes, he didn't seem to mind.

"How can I resist such a temptation?"

"Oh, I'm sure you could if you put your mind to it," she said.

"Why would I want to do that?" he asked.

"I'm standing right here," Cooper said. "Just waiting for my coffee and bear claw. It's nothing really. Don't mind me."

"I never do," the stranger said.

"You're not from around here," she said.

He shrugged and took out his wallet to pay. "Neither are you."

"Guilty," she said, putting their purchases in a brown bag since she hadn't opened the boxes yet. "I'm Canadian." She reached for the money and their hands touched. She felt the sizzle all the way to her toes and their gazes locked.

"Still standing here," Cooper said.

"You have a name?" she asked.

"Grant Boone. I'm visiting from Detroit."

She nodded. "I figured you were from somewhere in that region. The Midwestern accent without the patience or courtesies."

"That's so un-Canadian of you," he said.

"I've lived in New York the past couple of years."

"That'll do it. I enjoy a woman with an attitude every now and then."

"That's a shame," she said. "My attitude is pretty much like this all the time. I've got it on good authority that I'm a real pain in the ass."

"Ahh," Grant said, looking her over. "A man-hater. You've been wronged, darlin'?" He emphasized the word in a long drawl.

"Good grief," she heard Cooper mutter as he headed back toward the door.

"Who hasn't?" she asked, feeling the bitterness of Richard's betrayal rise up. "I didn't realize you were a psychic."

"Not a psychic," he said, rubbing at the scruff of his beard. "I'm a cop, which is pretty much the same thing."

"You don't look like any cop I've ever seen," she said. "What's a cop from Detroit doing in Surrender, Montana? I'm surprised you haven't keeled over from all the excitement here."

"I'm retired," he said, his face hardening to granite.

Well, well, she thought. She'd hit a sore spot.

"Retired? At your age?" she asked. "What are you, mid-forties? What'd you do?"

"That's a hell of a lot of questions from a stranger from Canada."

"What can I say?" she asked. "I'm a people person."

"Those are the kind of questions that should be answered over dinner," he said, smiling.

She almost rolled her eyes at the dimple that winked in one cheek. This guy was walking testosterone, and she wanted whatever he was selling. Then he turned his head and she saw the scarred flesh along his jaw that he'd kept hidden. Maybe he was testing her to see what her reaction would be. All she knew was that it didn't detract from him in any way. If anything, it just made him look more dangerous.

She was just about to suggest they skip dinner and go straight for dessert when the big square windows at the front of the bakery exploded and a hail of bullets ripped across the countertops and the glass showcase with all the baked goods.

Grant dove toward her and they flew through the air in what seemed like slow motion. She felt the impact to her head just as they landed with an *oomph* behind the counter. At the last second he turned so he didn't crush her beneath his weight.

Her vision was blurred and blackness was creeping in, but she heard him yell Cooper's name before she let the darkness take her.

Chapter Two

"Liza, you awake?"

The voice started like a small buzz in her ears, but got increasingly more annoying. Her head swam and nausea roiled in her belly.

"Goway," she slurred.

"Here, drink this."

She thought the voice was familiar, but she couldn't place it. Something cool touched her lips and she tried to swat it away, but the liquid splashed against her face and ran down her neck. Then she remembered. *Grant Boone*, the sexy retired cop with a chip on his shoulder and a body like a rock. She remembered because he'd landed on her and he'd been hard—*everywhere*.

"Ease off, Florence Nightingale," she rasped. "You're drowning me."

She strained to sit up, but the pain in her skull felt like someone was sticking daggers into her brain.

What the hell had happened? The mattress under her was soft and the sheets were cool and silky. The lights were dimmed, but she was very much aware that she was in someone's bedroom. Though she had no idea whose. If she'd had the courage, she would've checked to see if her clothes were still on.

"Did we have dessert?" she asked. "I don't normally drink. Is there anything I need to apologize for?"

"I think your brain is addled," he said. "You haven't been drinking. And we haven't had dessert. Here, take these."

He helped her sit up and she automatically put the two pills in her mouth and swallowed them down with the water. Her head was killing her, and the room was starting to spin. As soon as she swallowed the pills she laid down flat and closed her eyes.

"What happened?" she asked.

"Someone shot through…"

It all came crashing back and made her head hurt even worse. Her eyes widened with fear and she grasped his leg. "Gunshots! Ohmigod. Was I shot?"

She tried to assess the damage to her body, but the only thing that really hurt was her head. Had she been shot in the head?

"No, nothing as glamorous as that," he said. "You got hit in the head with a tray of donuts."

She lifted her hands and felt around for the knot on her head, wincing when she found it. "A tray of donuts?" she asked.

"Yep," he said, smiling for the first time since she'd opened her eyes, though it was strained.

"I don't mean to seem ungrateful," she started, "but I seem to be missing some time. The last thing I remember was you on top of me on the floor of the bakery. And now I'm in an unfamiliar bed with you looming over me. You can imagine my confusion."

"I can also appreciate your lack of hysterics. I'm not a fan."

"I'm not big on hysterics," she said. "But I'm pretty badass at revenge."

His hand slipped into hers and squeezed, and she felt the immediate relief of that human reassurance that everything was going to be okay. She could bravado her way through most situations, but she was scared and she had no clue what was going on. And then she remembered they weren't the only two in the bakery.

"Oh, God," she said. "Cooper? What happened?"

The jagged scar along his jaw turned white. He was pissed.

"He'll survive, but he took a hit."

"Jesus, poor Claire," she said, thinking of Cooper's wife. "She must be out of her mind with worry. I can't imagine."

"She's a cop's wife," he said. "It's their biggest fear come to life."

Liza had gotten to know Claire during her time in Surrender because Claire was the librarian, and sometimes she would walk across the street to the library when she closed at three o'clock and bring a few goodies that hadn't sold. They'd become friends, much to Liza's surprise. There was something about Claire that made Liza think she wasn't nearly as prim and proper as people thought she was.

"I feel like I'm having an out-of-body experience," she said. "This is Surrender. Things like this don't happen here. *Nothing* happens here."

"It's my fault," he said. "I didn't think she'd come here. I shouldn't have let Cooper go out and face her alone, but I had to make sure you were protected first."

"Her?" she asked.

Her head wasn't pounding quite as hard and she tried again to sit up against the headboard. Grant moved back to give her a little more room and leaned against the footboard, so he faced her.

"Ryan Caine," he said. "And it's a really long story. How about we table it for when your head doesn't feel like it's going to fall off?"

"It's feeling better now," she said. "Whatever was in those magic pills did the trick."

"Enjoy it while you can," he said. "They'll wear off soon enough and remind you a tray of donuts did you in."

"Hilarious," she said, deadpan.

His lips twitched and he took one of her feet in his hands. He gently pressed the arch of her foot and a moan escaped before she could help it. She'd be a fool to turn down a sexy guy giving her a foot rub, so she snuggled back down onto the bed and rested her head on the soft pillow.

"Let's just say someone from my former undercover life is a little pissed at me and looking for revenge. I'm not sure how she tracked me here. Since I retired, I've been doing some traveling. Lots of hiking and camping in remote locations and little cell service. I got a voicemail from Cooper a few days ago and he invited me to stay here for a while until I decide what I want to do."

"But this Ryan Caine found you?" she asked.

"She's good at what she does," he said. "Though she's never put civilians in harm's way before, but her desperation to kill me is making her reckless."

"Her desperation to kill you," she repeated, the immensity of those words sinking in. "What'd you do that made her want to kill you?"

"That's definitely a story for another time," he said.

"You've still not told me where we are." She sighed as his magic fingers worked their way up her calf and rubbed at the knot there.

"We're hiding, for the moment. We're in the apartment above the sheriff's office. Cooper had this place reinforced with bulletproof everything once his family's security business started drawing unsavory attention." Grant's voice was low, but his eyes scanned every corner and window of the room. "We're snug as two bugs for the time being."

His hands moved to her other foot and she arched her back, pushing against him as he dug at the sore muscles. She was very aware that she was alone in a bed with a man she'd just met. And somehow it didn't seem to matter. She knew it was the moment—the adrenaline of escaping danger and possibly death.

She also knew she would only be in Surrender long enough to settle her aunt's estate and sell the bakery, then she was heading to L.A. She had no particular ties to L.A., and she'd only visited a couple of times, but it was as far away from New York and Richard as she could get, so it seemed like a good move.

There was nothing wrong with being a little selfish every once in a while. With fulfilling wants and needs and throwing caution to the wind, especially when she'd just watched her life flash before her eyes. She was all of a sudden feeling very alive.

"Don't you want to take a closer look at my head?" she said, pouting and stroking the pillow next to her. "You didn't even kiss it to make it better."

He arched a brow and the corner of his mouth tilted up, and then he pushed her feet aside and crawled up next to her. "You're a world of trouble, Liza Carmichael."

"Life gets boring without a little trouble every now and then."

She saw the gleam in his eyes and knew he lived by the same philosophy. She'd been right when she'd told him she'd never seen a cop like him before. There was no way he put on a uniform every morning and lived by the book. He had *renegade* written all over him.

His body barely touched hers and the heat was unbelievable. She wasn't a woman who had one-night stands. In fact, she'd never had one at all. But something inside her was feeling wild and reckless, and she needed someone to cling to after the events of the day.

She realized then she wasn't the only one who needed the connection. She watched his pulse flutter in his throat. He was still amped up from the shooting.

He leaned over her and his lips gently touched the sore spot on her head, and then he lingered and breathed in her hair before touching his lips to her again.

Liza felt the pulse beneath his zipper, and she turned slightly to press against him. Her breasts felt heavy and she gasped as his arm came around her and his hand palmed her ass, squeezing gently.

"That body of yours has been taunting me since I saw you swearing at those boxes this morning. You'd probably run away if I told you what I'd like to do to that ass."

"Try me," she said. "Maybe you'd run screaming if you knew

what I wanted to do to your ass."

He barked out a laugh and jerked his shirt over his head, tossing it on the ground.

"Sweet Jesus," she said, making him laugh again.

His torso was a thing of legends. Never in her life had she seen abs so defined that they could've belonged to a sculpture. There was a light smattering of dark blond hair on his chest and his tattooed biceps bulged without him flexing. She stifled a giggle as the thought went through her mind that she was about to be ravished by Thor.

His hands went to the button on her jeans and snapped them open, and then he lowered the zipper before pulling them down her hips and thighs.

"You are round in all the right places, baby. I want to sink into that pussy so bad."

She sucked in a breath as he stripped her jeans the rest of the way off and dropped them on the floor in a heap.

"I can only imagine what those thighs will feel like around my waist," he said.

"You won't have to imagine if you'll hurry up," she panted. "Besides, I thought you were going to tell me what you're planning to do to my ass."

Before she realized it, he'd flipped her onto her stomach in a move that would've made Bruce Lee proud. He growled and his fingers stroked the round globe of her ass just before she felt the sting of his hand. Her fingers dug into the mattress and she let out a little yip of surprise. She felt the heat on her skin and the warmth between her legs.

"Again," she said, lifting her ass in the air.

"Like that, did you?"

"Oh, yeah. Do it again," she said, her voice more demanding this time.

"Bossy," he said, and then did as she asked, this time with three sharp smacks. "Red looks good on you, sweetheart."

She was soaking wet, and she whimpered as he leaned down

and kissed her reddened cheeks before he flipped her back over. His hands went to the buckle of his belt and the swish of it rushing through the belt loops had her eyes widening and her pussy spasming with anticipation.

"Naughty girl," he said, smirking.

"Apparently," she answered.

She pouted in disappointment as he put the belt on the nightstand and stripped out of his jeans. He most certainly wasn't shy, and he had no reason to be. She licked her lips in anticipation as his briefs joined his jeans on the floor.

"You're right," she said, voice raspy. "There's plenty of time for foreplay later. Very impressive."

"Take off your shirt," he ordered. "I'm afraid this first time is going to be fast and furious. I hope you don't mind."

She got up on her knees on the bed and pulled the clingy black shirt over her head so she was left in nothing but the lacy red underwear she'd put on that morning. She was an underwear junkie, and the sexier the better. She'd always worn it for herself first, but she was thanking God for her weakness at the moment because Grant looked like he was about to self-combust.

"Baby…" he said, coming onto the bed with her.

"Yes?"

"Those tits of yours are extremely fuckable."

"The rest of me is pretty fuckable too," she said, undoing the front clasp of her bra.

It had taken her a long time to feel comfortable in her own skin. To love her body. She'd never been like the other girls in school. She was six feet tall, for starters. And when you added curves to that it just made the teen years even more awkward. But she'd eventually learned that she'd never be a size zero, and she'd never be petite. Once she got her head out of the sand, she realized that men liked it when a woman could fill out her clothes in all the right places. Richard had always said she was "stacked." Of course, Richard was a horndog who couldn't keep his dick in his pants, so what did he know.

"I don't suppose you found any condoms in this place," she said, shrugging her bra off her shoulders and tossing it away.

"You should've looked under your pillow. There are four of them."

"Four?" she asked.

"I'm probably going to have to hunt up a few more than that," he said, facing her on his knees as well. "You are about the hottest thing I've ever laid eyes on. And I hope you don't mind, but…"

She gasped as he ripped the flimsy lace panties, and then his mouth was on hers in a kiss hotter than she'd ever experienced. She'd never been with a man his size, but men his size were rare. He had to be at least six foot four or five, and she actually had to tilt her head up to meet his lips.

She moaned and felt his cock press against her hip. It looked like they'd measure up perfectly. Hands roamed and legs tangled as they rolled across the giant bed. And then she felt him reach for the condom under the pillow and she watched him roll it on with a practiced hand.

His body came back down over hers, and the weight of him felt glorious as her legs circled his waist. She whimpered as he pressed into her, the size of him a shock to her system. And then he slid the rest of the way inside her in one smooth motion and she felt her eyes roll back into her head.

If someone had asked her to describe what being well and truly fucked felt like, she wouldn't have been able to do it. At least not coherently. It was like being outside her own body and being invaded at the same time. Heat infused her skin and the rhythmic glide of his cock against something deep inside of her made stars explode behind her closed eyes.

Her moans of pleasure grew louder and her nails bit into his back. And then he pushed against her once more—against that place inside of her that had never been touched. He held himself there.

And she lost her fucking mind.

Somewhere in the recesses of her brain she knew he was coming too, but she was too busy trying to breathe through the exquisite pleasure that wracked her body. She'd never had an orgasm that felt like it had been ripped from her very soul.

Sometime later, once the sweat had cooled from their skin and their hearts had stopped jackhammering against their chests, he managed to roll from her body, though he pulled her against him.

"That was nice," he said sleepily against her neck.

"Nice?" she asked, insulted. She'd just had the best sex of her life and he thought it was *nice?*

She felt his smile against her skin, and she stiffened against him. Maybe this was the reason she'd never had a one-night stand.

"Really nice," he amended and then laughed when she punched him in the arm. "You're already too cocky. I'm just trying to keep you level-headed."

"I should probably tell you that I'm not good at keeping a level head when I lose my temper. When I caught my ex-fiancé cheating on me, I might have driven my car through the bedroom window."

He jerked back in surprise. "I'm sleeping with a felon?"

"Nah, he didn't press charges. Rich people don't like the publicity, and it would've tarnished his golden-boy reputation if people found out he'd been screwing around on me. It was a win-win for everyone."

"I have to say the image of you driving through his bedroom window is kind of hot," he said. "Crazy. But hot."

"Sometimes justice needs to be served in ways that no cop or court can measure."

His expression hardened and he rolled to the side, disposing of the condom. "That I'll agree with a hundred percent."

Chapter Three

"Sure you're okay?" Grant asked. He pressed the phone against his ear and waited for Cooper to answer.

Cooper grunted and then there were muffled noises as someone else took the phone.

"Grant?" A familiar voice swept through the line.

"Who's this?" he asked, slightly distracted as he peeked through the blinds and looked out over Surrender. It was late afternoon and already the sun was disappearing behind the buildings across the street. He'd only stopped long enough to pull on his jeans as he'd gotten up to check the security of the apartment.

According to Lane Greyson, who was one of Cooper's deputies, Surrender hadn't seen this kind of violence and destruction since the late eighteen hundreds, back when Cole MacKenzie had been the only lawman in the territory.

Fast-forward a hundred and thirty years and once again, the people of Surrender had hidden in terror as gunfire destroyed a perfect piece of town history. Once the smoke had cleared and the shooter had vanished, the citizens of Surrender had swarmed Main Street, and even now there was still a crowd gathered in the street below. They'd be talking about the events of the morning a hundred years from now, just like they talked about what happened when Cole MacKenzie had to draw on his own brother more than a century before.

"It's Thomas," the voice said on the other end of the line.

Grant let the slat of the blind fall. Thomas MacKenzie was the town doctor, and he'd been able to tend to Cooper almost as soon as he'd been shot.

"What's up, Doc?" Grant asked.

"That never gets old," Thomas said dryly.

"I wouldn't care if it did," Grant grinned. "How's Coop?"

"He's fine. Already asking to be released, but he's going to be observed overnight. The perks of having MacKenzie Secur…"

"Don't tell me where you are," Grant interrupted. "There's a good possibility we're being monitored."

"Our family is used to it," Thomas said. "Tell the bastard to bring it on, whoever he is. Believe me, we've dealt with a lot worse."

"She," Grant said. "The bastard is a she."

"At least that makes it interesting," Thomas said. And then there was a lot of muttering and a couple of curses from Thomas. "Stop it, Coop. You're all drugged up. You are not leaving this bed. And no one is taking you out dancing. Claire would skin the both of us."

Grant chuckled as he listened to the conversation between the brothers and looked back at Liza, stretched out like a goddess on the bed. Damn, was that a sexy woman. She was still naked and barely covered by the sheet. Statuesque was what his father would've called her. And she was in crazy good shape. He'd probably have bruises on his lower back where her heels had pressed in.

Grant moved back to the bed and slid in behind her, wrapping his arm around her.

"We should give Coop drugs more often," Thomas said, laughing. "He's kept the whole family laughing with his gibberish."

"Like what?"

"He keeps talking about an assassin and a hellcat. And then says women are nothing but trouble."

"That's the damned truth," he said.

"That's part of the reason I wanted to talk to you," Thomas said. "Before I shot Cooper full of drugs, he said you need to get out of town and lay low. Whoever's after you doesn't seem to care that there are a lot of innocent bystanders in her way."

"No, not this time," Grant said. "I'll draw her away."

"I have a remote cabin up in the mountains we use during hunting season. I'll text you the location. Oh, and Coop said don't get too caught up with the hellcat. She's trouble with a capital *T*."

Cooper had tried to warn him off before, but now that he'd felt that body wrapped around him, the warnings were starting to piss him off.

"Why?" Grant bit the word out.

"Well, rumor has it she drove a Mercedes through her fiancé's house."

"Ex-fiancé," he corrected. "And I knew that already. Tell me something I don't know."

"Since he knows you're drawn to trouble like a fly to honey, he also said to tell you the apartment above the sheriff's office has cameras strategically located throughout, but he wants you to know they're not activated. It was Cooper's place before he got married."

Which explained everything. He and Cooper had been friends long enough that he knew exactly the kind of lifestyle Cooper had led before marriage. Hell, Grant had even joined him at the clubs he'd enjoyed a time or two.

"I guess that would explain the pulley system over the bed," he said.

"Oh, yeah," Thomas said, drawing out the words. "And, it's…"

"Remote control," Grant finished for him. "I've already figured it out and have great plans for it."

"I'm not at all surprised. You and Cooper are two of a kind."

"Except he still has a job," Grant said, the bitterness escaping more than he'd meant it to.

"A job for now," Thomas said. "You never know what opportunities await once you get out of your comfort zone."

"Yeah, yeah." He sighed and then looked down at his phone as it buzzed. "Got your text of the location. We'll head out after nightfall."

"In all seriousness," Thomas said, "be careful. From what I understand, this woman almost got you once. All you need to do is ask for help and it's yours. You're like a brother to Coop, and we take that seriously."

"I've got it," he said. "I can handle a damn woman. I had her once, and I'll have her again."

Liza turned in his arms and her gaze narrowed on his before she tried to buck out of his hold.

"Not you," he mouthed.

"Be careful out there," Thomas said. "And call if you need reinforcements. Oh, and don't let her drive." Thomas was laughing when Grant hung up on him.

"What's all that about?"

"Nothing much. You know Thomas?"

"Anyone who's ever spent any amount of time in Surrender knows all of the MacKenzies. It's hard not to," she said, smirking. "They make an impressive package. And it didn't sound like nothing."

"He told me I shouldn't let you drive."

"That's not the first time I've heard that," she said. "What do you think, cowboy? You think driving a car through someone's house makes me a crazy bitch?"

"Some people might think that," he said. "But there's something to be said for that level of betrayal. You've got a wild streak. He should've known that after being engaged to you. Hell, I've known you a few hours and I already know that. I happen to like wild streaks."

"That would explain the damn woman you said you could

handle," she said, arching a brow. "Can I assume that's who shot the hell out of my bakery this morning?"

"That would be a good assumption," he said. "We really need to get out of here."

"Why? I thought you said this place was safe."

"It's bulletproof," Grant said, hesitating. "But maybe not safe. And there's also the issue of the cameras in this place."

She recoiled and her gaze darted around the room, looking for any visible signs.

"And no, I didn't know about them beforehand," he said before she could ask. "This used to be Cooper's place, and let's just say he was into doing things a little differently."

"I'd always heard the rumors about Cooper and his sexual tastes when I was growing up, but I never thought they were a hundred percent true. You know how people in small towns like to talk."

"Oh, they're true," Grant said. "Cooper took his role as a Dom very seriously."

"What about you?" she asked, walking her fingers across his thigh. "Do you share any of his kinks?"

"I've been known to," he said. "But more for recreation. It was never a lifestyle for me."

"I'll keep that in mind," she said, rolling from the bed and heading out of the room, naked as a jaybird.

He wasn't sure what that was supposed to mean. Was she turned off by the thought of adding a little kink to sex? Women were a damned mystery. He got out of bed and followed behind her like a damned whipped puppy. He already wanted to get his hands on her again.

She walked through the living room and toward the kitchen, and the outside motion lights came on.

"Get down," he told her, pushing her to the floor in case she got a stubborn streak and decided not to listen.

"What's going on?" she whispered, struggling to be released.

"Caine," he said.

"I've got to tell you I'm not a fan," she said. "She seems like a real bitch."

"That would be an accurate assessment. The motion lights outside just came on. The windows here are bulletproof, but I'd prefer not to test the theory if we can keep from it."

"Right," she said, and then her eyes got big as saucers as he pulled out his 9mm and pointed it toward the door.

"Where'd you have that thing hidden?"

"Don't ask," he said. "Look, we can access Cooper's office through the trapdoor under the living room rug. There's a drop-down set of stairs. The only problem is the downstairs isn't reinforced like it is up here, so we'll be exposed. But at least we can grab keys to one of his units and get the hell out of here."

"No way, Lieutenant Bad Ass," she hissed. "I'm not sneaking into a sheriff's office to escape like a criminal. Why don't you just call in backup?"

"This is Surrender. Cooper is in the hospital and drugged out of his mind and there's one deputy on duty. Every town around us has the same small police force. It's going to take time to gather a task force with enough numbers to go after her. At least a couple of days. So there is no backup right now.

"And we're not sneaking. I have permission to access whatever I need to." Their voices were still hushed. He couldn't hear any footsteps outside. The place was soundproofed, which worked in both their favors. "Lane Greyson said he'd give us a hand as soon as he could when I talked to him, but he's dealing with some cows that managed to escape their enclosure. One of them walked into the road and caused a car to go into the ditch, and another one was found destroying some lady's garden."

"Wow," she said. "I'm guessing that kind of police work is unique to here."

"You'd be surprised," he said. "Cops out here have to be well trained. There's a lot of open space, and it's a great area for major drug crimes and fugitives. Surrender has experienced both, and they're damned lucky to have Cooper as their sheriff."

He motioned for her to stay down and he quietly rolled to his feet, making his way toward the window closest to the door. The landing area was small, and there wasn't a place to hide. If she was out there, then he'd see her. He carefully shifted the blinds and felt his pulse spike when a cat jumped from the banister onto the porch and then ran back down the stairs.

"Cat," he said, letting out a slow breath.

"Jesus," she said, rolling onto her back. "Too many highs and lows in a day. This adrenaline rush shit is no joke."

"I can help you with that, sugar."

She tilted her head up and stretched seductively. "Oh, yeah? What's the cure?"

"It's a step-by-step program," he said, setting his gun on the coffee table. The motion light blinked off and he was left standing in almost total darkness. Only the dim light from the gaslights down Main Street eased between the edges of the window that looked over the town.

"What's step one?" she asked, rolling back to her hands and knees. He unsnapped the button of his jeans, his erection throbbing behind the zipper, and he pushed them down around his hips so his cock sprang free.

"Crawl over here, sweetheart. I've been dying to see those sexy lips stretched around my dick."

He watched her crawl toward him, and the closer she got the harder his dick spiked. She stopped in front of him and sat up on her knees, resting her hands on his thighs.

"Mmm," she said, licking her lips. And then she took him in her mouth and his knees wanted to buckle.

He twisted her hair in his fist and pulled her head back slightly, so her mouth opened further. And then he slowly stretched her to her limits, her tongue undulating against the underside of his cock as her throat opened and she swallowed him whole.

"Holy shit, Liza," he rasped. He wasn't a small man, but she took him down with ease, and it was everything he could do not to shoot all he had straight down her throat.

She gasped for breath when he pulled out, but she was ravenous, swirling her tongue around the head before taking him down again. At the pace she was going, holding back wouldn't be an issue.

"If I don't fuck you now, I'm going to come down your throat."

He felt her smile against the head of his cock, and he jerked as she gave him a quick lick.

"We don't want that," she said. "At least not right now. I'm in a selfish mood, and I want you inside me."

He kept his grasp on her hair as he guided her to the position he wanted, so she was on all fours in front of him.

"Don't move," he said, and released his grip.

"You're very demanding," she said. "I don't like being bossed around."

He rolled on a condom and moved behind her, taking hold of her hair again. And then he leaned forward and whispered in her ear, "You like it," he said. "Because you're still exactly where I put you. And you know I'm about to give you the fucking of a lifetime."

He pushed inside of her with one stroke and she bucked beneath him. And then she went wild, pushing back against his every thrust. Her cries grew louder, and he was ever thankful of Cooper's foresight in having the place soundproofed, because there was no doubt in his mind that people on the street would be hearing her otherwise.

He felt his balls tighten and she gasped in pleasure as he grew larger inside her. He dropped down over her, like a stallion mounting a mare, and he bit lightly on her shoulder.

"You asked if I had any kinks," he whispered. "I've got a few."

Her pussy spasmed around him and he felt her orgasm approaching. "Like what?"

"I'm not going to wait much longer to fuck that sweet ass,"

he said. "You ever had a three-way, baby?"

He didn't know why he was pushing her. He didn't particularly care for three-ways, and the thought of sharing Liza with anyone made him irrationally angry. But there was a war raging inside of him that was caused by one woman, and he could feel himself slipping under her spell. She fascinated him. And he couldn't seem to get enough of her.

He felt her hesitation at the question, but he kept pushing.

"No," she said softly.

"What do you think, baby?" he asked. "You want to know what pleasure is? I can just imagine watching you ride someone else, that sweet ass rising up and down."

She whimpered and he felt the small fluttering of pulses around his cock. He nipped her shoulder once more, this time a little harder.

"I'd crawl up behind you and take your ass," he said. "Can you imagine how full you'd be as we slid in and out of you? I'm telling you there's nothing like it. There's nothing like having two dicks come deep inside of you."

"Fuck," she growled and threw her head back. Her pussy squeezed so tight around him it jerked the orgasm from his body.

Liza collapsed beneath him, and he didn't have the strength this time to even roll to the side.

Chapter Four

It was close to three in the morning. Showered, but approaching the point of going way beyond his second wind, Grant knew he had to remain more alert than ever before. If Ryan Caine had planned to launch an attack, it would be at this time of the morning. It was a vulnerable period.

Grant looked at a sleeping Liza and decided not to disturb her until he had worked out a final escape plan. Sitting on the hand-scraped wooden floor, he peered through a gap in the window. His Colt AR15 rifle rested against the window's sill, and his 9mm semiautomatic pistol was shoved back in his jeans.

There were too many places to hide for Caine to set up a sniper's nest. He knew she was one of the best long-gunners in the game. Grant had personally trained her. They were both assigned to a special tactical task force in the Detroit metro area when they'd first met. Actually, he'd done more than train her to become a weapons expert. They'd been lovers for more than a year before she'd betrayed him.

Caine had become entangled with the notorious gang leader Eduardo Diaz. Caine had teetered dangerously over the thin blue line. Life along the fringes of society fueled her addiction for risk. Diaz fed that need and lured her over to the dark side. It happened to a lot of cops. But not all cops were as well trained as

Caine was.

For Lieutenant Grant Boone, there'd been no gray area where upholding the law was concerned. It was either black or white. Caine had gone too far, and he'd not had any regrets turning her into Detroit PD's Internal Affairs Division. They'd had sex and nothing deeper. He'd never go against his own moral code to protect a snake like her, even though he knew what it was like to be intimate with her.

She'd gone on the run with Diaz, mocking the police at every turn, committing crimes just so she and her new lover could watch the police try and prove it was them. They were the king and queen of Detroit's underground crime syndicate. The worst of the worst. They had money, political influence, and power.

And then the two of them had gotten married in a fairy-tale wedding that covered the front page of every newspaper in the state and some of the surrounding ones. But Grant hadn't stopped looking for a way to bring them down. He knew the key was to bring down Diaz first. He was the one who was *really* in charge.

Caine excelled at her specific skill set, but when it came to commanding men, she didn't have the charisma that made others want to follow. Diaz's men were loyal because he took care of them, and in his own way, he cared about them. Caine didn't share those same sentiments. She cared about herself first and foremost, but her new husband was a close second.

Diaz was a brilliant businessman, but he had one weakness. Ryan Caine. And the reason he was in prison was because of her. She'd wanted more—more money, more power, more everything—and he'd tried to give it to her. And that's how Grant nailed him.

They'd caught him brokering an arms deal himself. Usually deals like that were months in the making, and he had men in place to play decoy and confuse the cops. And he never appeared in person to do the deals, but would send one of his right-hand men.

Caine had convinced him to take a risky deal, and Diaz had

agreed. And when the cops had raided the warehouse, Diaz had returned fire and taken out a rookie officer who'd never see his twenty-third birthday. Diaz had been wounded in the exchange, but satisfaction had come with Diaz's life sentence.

It had sent Caine right over the edge. She didn't have the respect that Diaz had, so their organization had crumbled pretty rapidly. She'd vowed revenge against Grant, deciding he was the only one to blame, and she'd done everything in her power to exact it on him.

He hadn't taken her threats idly.

"What caused this?" a voice asked from the shadows.

He jerked with a hand wrapped around the butt of his pistol. Liza had surprised him. He hadn't heard her waken. He'd been lost in the past.

"What do you mean?"

She came toward him and he saw she'd found a thin robe to put on. Even after he'd had her multiple times, his body hardened for her again. She sat on the sofa and nodded at his weapons.

"You're a natural predator, Grant. A dangerous and capable individual. I sensed it, and while there are aspects of you that frighten me some, I also know you've got an agenda based on your own sense of duty and what's right. She's a threat and you're not going to stop until she's taken down. This is my life too. I want to know what's going on."

"It's good old revenge. I locked up her murdering husband—for life."

"And?" Liza asked impatiently.

"And then she almost killed me."

"And?" she taunted.

"And then I destroyed everything she and that piece of shit ever created."

"Okay, just so this doesn't drag on all night, at what point did you fuck her? Before or after she turned criminal?"

He cut his eyes sideways and looked at her stubborn expression. Liza Carmichael was no fool.

"Before," he said. "We were partners in a special task force. I trained her to be as stealthy as she is lethal. We dominated the city's drug scene, and enjoyed every moment of doing it together. She was a natural, but not everyone can handle the pressure. She became as addicted to the danger as the criminals were to the drugs and money."

"Did you stay with her after she turned?"

"For a little while," he confessed. "Mostly so I could gather enough evidence, but there was still a part of me that hoped I could bring her back. Then she ran across Diaz. He fed her desire for violence and chaos, and it wasn't long before they were being seen in public together. I had no choice. I'd not only lost her to him, but she'd lost all sense of good and bad. There was nothing *but* bad left."

"How'd you finally catch her?" she asked.

"I caught her trying to destroy the evidence we'd amassed against Diaz. IA got involved, and she was toast. After that, there was nothing stopping her crime and killing sprees, especially combining her talents with Diaz. She's a bad apple, Liza—the worst."

"I hope you don't mind my asking, but what happened that you were forced to retire?"

He knew that question would come. Liza was a woman full of questions. She was curious, and she wasn't stupid. She was also pretty damned observant, and he knew it wouldn't be long before she started putting bits of overheard conversation together.

"She went crazy the first couple of months after Diaz was captured and sent to prison. She set my apartment building on fire and trashed my car. My captain decided to bring me in from undercover and stick me behind a desk until she was caught, and he put me in charge of a task force to bring her in.

"It was a Wednesday, and I was in plainclothes, though I had to wear a jacket and tie instead of my usual biker clothes, and I was sitting at my desk with the phone to my ear. I had a tennis ball I was tossing up and catching while I talked on the phone to an informant. If I hadn't dropped the ball, I'd be dead. I swiveled in my chair to lean down and get it just as she pulled the trigger. She's a hell of a sniper. Snagged me in the shoulder from almost a mile away, right into the fucking police station.

"After I got out of the hospital, I went after her," he said unapologetically. "Full fucking force. I blasted and burned down everything I knew she had her fingers in."

"Why didn't she go to jail?" she asked.

"Why didn't you go to jail when you drove that car through your fiancé's house?" he countered. His past was never easy for him to talk about.

She shrugged and played with the tie on her robe. "He was rich. Like, really rich. With political aspirations. The last thing he wanted was a scandal, so I packed my stuff, he dealt with covering up what had happened, and I took the red BMW as a consolation prize. My turn to ask a question," she said. "How'd Cooper end up in Detroit?"

"He'd come on as a temporary task force agent. He was hunting a fugitive believed to be connected to Diaz's crew. After we'd snatched him, the guy gave info about a hit attempt on my life by none other than Ryan Caine. The guy was Cooper's snitch, but I think Cooper assumed the rat was just trying to rattle his cage to cook an immunity deal or block extradition. Cooper figured it was bullshit. Less than six hours later I was gasping through an opening beneath my jaw big enough to stick my hand through. And I ended up in the hospital again.

"The chief thought my aggressive tendencies to bring her in would eventually get me killed, and he was concerned about the psychological damage he thought she might have done during our relationship. He wanted me in counseling to make sure everything was okay. I refused, and IA trumped up a bunch of bullshit about acting outside my authority in trying to bring her in, and I was given the opportunity to retire. It's a hell of a way to end a twenty-five year career."

"Wow," she said, brows raising. "And you and Cooper are

still friends?"

"We were friends long before that. I think that's what causes him the most guilt. But it's part of the job. That gut instinct. And snitches are always looking out for themselves first. There's no such thing as a trustworthy snitch."

"Do you resent him?"

"We've got too deep a history for that," Grant said. "Mistakes happen in our line of work. There are many times those mistakes lead to death. I got lucky that day."

"I'm glad you're not carrying around that kind of hate. Especially toward a friend."

"I didn't know you cared, sugar," he said.

"There's better ways to use energy than by hating someone."

"Like revenge?" he asked.

She lowered her gaze and continued to play with the tie of her robe. "Yeah, well, revenge is short lived." Then she looked up and smiled. "But damn can it be satisfying."

Grant answered her smile and stood. "It's late enough," he said. "It's time to get out of here. I don't suppose I can convince you to let me drop you at the MacKenzies and have you stay there?"

"Not a chance," she said. "That bitch shot up my bakery. Do you know how expensive it's going to be to get it fixed up before I can put it on the market?"

"Still planning on taking off, huh?" he asked.

She shrugged. "What else am I supposed to do? I've got no family left. I've got no one. All I have is a little house outside of town and a bakery with a bunch of holes in it."

"Right," he said.

"I haven't heard you talking about any big plans for your retirement," she said a little sharply.

"I'm retired," he said. "I don't have to have any big plans. Coop wants me to stay here awhile. Maybe take one of the deputy positions. I'm thinking about it."

To be honest, he didn't know what the hell to do with

himself. He'd had the years to retire and draw his full pension, so he'd taken it. But he wasn't the kind of man who could sit idle for very long, especially since most of his career had been fast-paced and adrenaline inducing. Staying in Surrender would definitely be a change of pace, but Cooper had said there were occasions when extra help was needed at MacKenzie Security, and that was something that definitely intrigued him.

"Do you have a plan to get us out of here?" she asked.

"No, not so much," he said. "Still got your Beemer keys?"

"Yes," she said, drawing out the word. "Do you want them?"

"That would be helpful. I know she's out there. I just need a little bait."

"Umm… That's an eighty-thousand-dollar car."

"Good thing you didn't pay for it," he countered.

"True, but still. It's the principle of the thing."

"How much is your life worth?"

Liza sighed. "I don't suppose you retrieved my purse after I got hit in the head with the tray of donuts."

"No, but one of the ladies grabbed it and brought it over when I carried you here. It's on the counter."

She went to retrieve the red leather bag from the counter and dug the keys from inside it.

"By the way," he said. "I'm pretty much going to tell the donut story to everyone I see. It's the best."

"Seriously?"

"Oh, yeah. Gossip like that is gold in a place like Surrender."

"Lovely," she said, handing him the keys. "Now what?"

"Well, let's talk facts. I know she's out there with a military grade, Barrett M107, 50 caliber recoil-operated, semiautomatic sniper rifle. It's a fucking sexy weapon. The night scope alone allows her to see the cheese on the moon."

"How do you know for sure?" she asked. "Maybe we can just make a run for it."

"I trained her. That's how I know for sure. If you want to run, then run. She won't kill you."

His assumption surprised her. "Why wouldn't she kill me?"

"I didn't say she wouldn't shoot you. I just said she wouldn't kill you. If she wounds you, she'd know I'd come out of hiding long enough to pull you to safety."

He was protective by nature. It was part of the job that he'd lived and breathed for the past twenty-five years. But the thought of Liza getting hurt shook him to his core. And if he was being honest with himself, he didn't know if he could keep her safe.

"So I'm bait?" she asked.

"Yep. Still want to run for it? If she shoots you with that rifle, it'll take a leg off. That thing is serious business."

"I'm good, thanks."

"Good call. Now go get dressed. I've already been through every cabinet and cupboard in this place to see if there's anything we could use. It looks like Claire and Cooper kept an extra change of clothes here. You might want to trade those boots out for tennis shoes, if they fit. And a sweatshirt. Nights are still cold."

She nodded, her expression serious. He could see the worry and fear in her eyes. This wasn't the kind of life she was used to. She'd spent however long being the pampered fiancé of a millionaire who baked cookies on the side for fun. This was a whole different level of adventure.

He followed her into the bedroom and did the same. He laced up his boots and stuck his knife in the sheath down inside it. He didn't bother layering more than a black T-shirt and a dark flannel shirt. He didn't want anything hampering his movements. He needed every advantage he could get dealing with Caine and keeping Liza safe too.

He went back into the living room and checked the windows once more to see if there was any movement.

"All right," she said, coming out of the bedroom, her purse strapped across her body.

"I want you to press the unlock button on your key fob. If we're lucky, she'll think we're running for safety and pop a long-range round into the car."

"Seriously, it's an eighty-thousand dollar car."

"I know. You mentioned it. Ready?"

Grant stabilized his observation position and looked through the scope of his rifle—the same rifle she was using.

"We'll have to move fast," he told her. "And this is one time when you need to follow instructions."

She narrowed her eyes at him and put a hand to her hip. "I'm not an idiot. I can take instruction when needed. Now let's move on so you don't stick your other foot in your mouth."

Grant grunted and turned back to the window and his rifle. There was no need for him to watch the BMW still parked crooked at the side of the bakery. His focus was on the elevated foothills.

He opened his eyes wide to allow his vision to clear. There were four potential shooting plateaus that he would have selected. He practiced scanning across all four of the spots where Caine might be without allowing his head to travel too far before springing back. That would waste the precious few seconds he'd have to spot her immediately.

"Make sure you press the unlock button."

"Got it," she said.

"Now."

Grant made sure to focus his glare away from the BMW's tail and interior lights. He'd adjusted his vision to see through the night, and the flashing car would've diminished it. He heard the double beep as soon as she hit the button.

He bore down against the high-powered scope—his breath trapped deep in his chest so his movements stayed steady. He was like a stone statue. But there was nothing at plateau one…or two…or three. His heart sank—she wasn't out there.

"Wait," he hissed. "I see her."

Liza pressed her back to the wall. "Where? Can you get a shot off?"

"I saw a reflection from the lens on her scope. She's on the third plateau. From this window, she's at exactly three o'clock.

She's not in a position where I'm comfortable taking a shot."

"What do we do?"

"Time to blow this popsicle stand." He put his hand on her shoulder. "I'm really sorry you got mixed up in this, but I'm not sorry for the time we've spent together."

"No regrets," she agreed. "But next time you want to get in my pants, just ask. No need to spice things up with an assassin. I didn't realize that's what you meant about kinky sex."

He snorted out a laugh and opened the square hatch hidden under the rug in the living room that led down to the sheriff's office below. "Baby, you haven't seen kinky yet. Now get that sweet ass down the ladder and let's get the hell out of here."

Chapter Five

They made it downstairs to the sheriff's office and took the keys from the hook behind the receptionist's desk. There was enough light for them to find their way, and like Grant said, it was essential to get out of town and draw Caine's attention away from innocent bystanders. She'd been worried that Deputy Greyson might come back to the sheriff's office and start flipping lights on. He'd be a prime target. But Grant had assured her that he'd told the deputy to steer clear of downtown.

Liza's skin tingled with adrenaline. She'd always been a thrill seeker, but this was a little more than she'd bargained for. In less than twenty-four hours she'd been shot at and had the best sex of her life. Now she was on the run. There was no guarantee if she stayed behind with the MacKenzies that this Caine woman wouldn't come after her. Just the fact that she'd been with Grant might be enough to put her on the assassin's radar.

"Seriously?" she said, looking at the keys to the vehicle he'd selected. "Do you want us to get caught?"

"It's exactly what we need," he said, holding onto the old Bronco keys. "It doesn't have a remote start and that thing is built to be durable and go over some rough terrain. Plus, it's still a police vehicle, so we can haul ass if we need to."

"I'm just saying, someone needs to do something about the

police budget around here and update the vehicles," she said.

"That's pretty much what all police budgets look like, rich girl," he said, rolling his eyes. "But maybe that's something you can advocate for if you decide to stick around. You seem like you'd be one of those people who likes making waves in the community."

"I'm not rich," she said. "My ex-fiancé was rich. There's a big difference. When I left to come to Surrender, all I had was my clothes, the car, and what was in my savings account. Every month I'd withdraw cash from the allowance account he'd set up for me, and I'd deposit it into the savings account. Just in case."

"Trusting soul, aren't you?"

"In hindsight, no. I never trusted Richard. It was just a niggling feeling in my gut. I had a successful online business when I was in Canada. I sold novelty cakes and pastries. It was a booming business, and it still pisses me off I sold my house and that amazing kitchen because Richard wanted me to move to New York and become a politician's wife. He told me it would look better if I established myself and eventually opened a respectable bakery, but not until the kids were in school."

"Novelty cakes?" he asked. "What's a novelty cake?"

"You know those cupcakes that are shaped like boobs? Those were very popular. I shipped them all over the world."

"Boob cupcakes," he said.

Liza felt her back stiffen. She'd always been very proud of her work, but there were some people too prudish to realize there was an art behind it. "Yeah, boob cupcakes. You disapprove?" she asked, her voice sharp.

"Not at all," he said, looking surprised. "I was just trying to imagine walking into the bakery and seeing boob cupcakes on the shelf. It might take a little getting used to in a place like Surrender. But Cooper told me his sister-in-law sells intimate items in the back room of her clothing boutique, so maybe y'all could work something out."

"I had no idea she was selling that kind of stuff here in

town," she said. "I've been so busy with the bakery I haven't really had a chance to do much of anything else." But it was most definitely something to think about. She didn't have a plan for her life. Not really. And there was no telling how long it might take to sell the bakery, especially now that it was in the condition it was in. She doubted there was a swarm of people looking to open businesses in a small town like Surrender.

"You ready?" he asked.

"Not really, but what the hell? Let's do it anyway."

"If we get to where we're going alive, I promise to make it worth your while," he said, patting her butt.

"I'm going to hold you to it. And it had better be chandelier-swinging sex."

"Sex?" he said innocently. "I was just going to cook you dinner."

She laughed and felt some of the tension drain from her shoulders, and then she nodded that she was ready to go.

He unlocked the back door and handed her the keys, and she paused, looking nervous. "Tell me why we're doing this again? Why can't we wait for help?"

"Because the closest town is an hour away and it's smaller than Surrender, and all the trained MacKenzie agents are out on assignment. And we're leaving this building because Caine likes to set fire to things and watch them burn. It's only a matter of time before she does the same to us. Our best bet is to escape and lose her on the way to Thomas's cabin. We'll need to hide the car along the way and walk in. Hopefully, we'll lose her in the mountains. The trees are thick and will give good cover. She won't be able to track us properly until daylight, but at least innocent bystanders will be safe, and it gives a little more time for a backup team to be put together and arrive."

"Right," she said. "I'm not liking our odds."

"I've had worse. Now go quickly and stay hunkered down so you're a smaller target. I'll cover you best I can. If you hear shots, get in that Bronco and drive. Understand?"

She nodded and then waited for his command.

"Go," he said.

She did as he said and found her hands shook as she tried to unlock the passenger side door. The click of the lock as it opened was the best sound she'd ever heard. And then she hit the button to unlock the driver's side.

Grant scooted in and laid the rifle between them. "Hold on," he said. "We're going to do this quick."

Liza's heart pounded in her chest and she sucked in deep breaths. Her fingers were white-knuckled around the *oh-shit* bar as she stared through the window, waiting for the attack to come. The ignition caught and the engine revved as she felt the Bronco lurch into gear.

"Get down," Grant yelled.

There was a roaring in her ears and Liza caught a glimpse of Grant's right hand coming toward her, pushing her down. The windshield exploded, and tiny pieces of glass rained down on her.

"Ohmigod, ohmigod, ohmigod," she chanted as she squeezed her quivering body against the door.

Grant kept his head down and his foot pressed on the pedal. The solid-body Bronco roared from the parking spot and bounced as Grant drove over parking barriers and curbs. Bullets rained in from the front and then through the driver's side door.

Liza felt the heat of tears against her cheeks and a fear unlike anything she'd ever known take over her. She waited for Grant's instructions and any indication he'd been injured. She held her breath as Grant sat up to see where he was going.

"You can sit up, but stay slouched in the seat as best you can."

She nodded because her voice wasn't working, and then she stared down at her shaking hands. What had just happened wasn't really processing, and she had a pretty good feeling she was in shock.

Then she looked over at Grant and felt her stomach roll. He was covered in blood, and it was flowing freely from the cuts on his face and head. She brought her hand up and brushed the shards of glass from his hair and shoulders.

"I don't understand what just happened. I thought you said you saw her in the foothills? How'd she get to us so quickly?"

Liza pressed her hand over her mouth because it came out as more of an accusation than a question.

"She set us up. She's anticipating my moves."

"Just what does that mean?"

Grant's face was dark and menacing. "It means this is going to suck."

"At least the Bronco is still…"

On cue, steam erupted from beneath the hood. It was a miracle that only the radiator had been torn apart by her shooting.

"Fuck," he said, slapping his hand against the steering wheel. "She did that on purpose. Laid down fire for fun to watch us scramble, and then she put one shot through the radiator so we'd end up stranded. It's always a fucking game to her. And now she can hunt us. Climb in the back and see if there's anything we can use. We've got to get moving. The directions Thomas sent are about ten miles from here."

"Ten miles?" Liza asked. "But you're injured."

"It's not the injuries or the distance that'll kill us, it's the screwing around out here that will. Let's move," Grant demanded, getting out of the car.

She crawled into the back and looked around. "There's nothing here but a few roadside flares."

She was glad Grant had suggested the tennis shoes and sweatshirt. It was cold, and would only get colder as they were out in the elements. And there was still snow in the higher elevations.

Grant grunted and started moving in a northeast direction. Liza shoved the flares in her purse and followed after him.

"Are you going to tell me what happened back there?" she asked.

"She's better than when I trained her," he said. "She set up her scope to look like a rifle's shooting platform. She knew that flattening the glass lenses directly toward the apartment window would cast a glare. I fell for it. I never looked beyond the glint of light to confirm she was behind the scope. I was in too damn big of a hurry. Or I was distracted by you."

"So she still has her long-range rifle?"

Grant stopped and looked at her briefly. "Yeah, but the good news is, she left her scope on that rock."

"What if she had two scopes?"

He stared at her and then kept walking.

"Sorry," she said. "Just thought I'd mention that."

He grunted again and picked up the pace. About a mile and a half into the forced march, Liza stumbled and fell to her knees. She was tired, cold, and she couldn't see shit. But Grant was there immediately and helped her back to her feet.

"I'm fine," she said. "I've got it."

"I never suggested otherwise," he said. "You know, it's okay for people to help you. You don't have to do everything on your own."

"I've always done everything on my own. I don't know any other way."

"That's an interesting insight," he said.

"Not really. It is what it is." She walked off a little way to make sure she hadn't twisted something important. There was a long way to go. She yanked her cell phone from her bag. "This is ridiculous. It's twenty-first century America. There's got to be someone we can call for help."

Grant pressed her activation button and showed her there was no signal. "This might be twenty-first century America, but it's also Surrender, Montana. Help has been called. But it takes time. We have to have people who are trained in this terrain and are familiar with tracking someone like Caine. They'll be able to find her a hell of a lot easier than I can because I know jack shit about Montana territory, so our best option is to find that cabin and hold her off as long as we can until the cavalry arrives."

"Why doesn't she just kill us? She's had all day to try and get in upstairs or burn us out. Why's she waiting?" she asked as she continued to follow him across the rough terrain. The temperature had dropped and their elevation had increased.

Grant's breath came out in white puffs, but he didn't seem tired. In fact, she would've said the opposite. He looked energized. She hated to think what she looked like at the moment, but it probably wasn't good.

"It's a game to her." He swigged from a bottle of water and then passed it to her. "It's always been a sick, twisted game. From the time I spent training her to when she seduced me and eventually betrayed me. It's easy to see in hindsight."

"But you were thinking with the wrong head?" she said sweetly.

He cut her a look. "Something like that. She could've picked off either of us back there. She's allowing you to live so you'll slow me down."

"I'm your anchor?" Liza asked, wishing she could muster up the courage to be insulted, but she knew it was true.

He grinned as she passed the water back. "Don't worry, sugar. You're not too heavy."

"I'm so relieved," she said dryly.

Something howled and she shivered as Grant picked up the pace. She wasn't a country girl. She had no idea if it was the wind she was hearing or a mountain lion. Or if Montana even had mountain lions.

She'd also never really understood what true darkness was until she'd come to Montana. Even in downtown Surrender there were still streetlights, and her neighbors left their porch lights on. Wherever they were now, the absence of light was absolute. Not the sliver of moon or the few stars in the sky could light a darkness that vast.

The ground was uneven, the roots from trees sticking above ground to act as tripwire. The rocks and loose dirt made some of the inclines almost impossible to grab a foothold.

"Shit," he whispered. "Do you see that?"

It took a minute for her eyes to adjust, but there in the distance she saw it. A single bouncing light. Immediately her gut went on high alert. It was as if Caine was using the light to tease them, like one would do with a penlight to taunt a cat.

"I really hate this woman," Liza muttered.

"Join the club. At least you didn't sleep with her."

"That's true. There's no accounting for taste."

"Nice," he said. "I'm taking left. I want you to take right. Let's split ourselves as targets and make it harder on her. Go exactly fifty paces and find cover. I'll find you once I've gotten a better hold on her position. I'm willing to bet she's using some kind of reflector on that light to make it seem like she's in a different location."

Liza swallowed hard. "You want to split up?" she asked, the sick knot of dread returning to her stomach. She was a baker for Christ's sake. Not G.I. Jane.

"You'll be fine. The probability of her being in that general direction is a lot smaller than the way I'm going. I'm going to try and draw her attention to me."

"Right," she said. "Fifty paces."

He grabbed her hand before she could take off. "You're doing good, baby. Real good. I'm proud of you." Then he squeezed her hand and he was gone.

Had anyone ever told her that in her entire life? Her parents certainly hadn't. Maybe her aunt had a time or two when she'd helped at the bakery in the summer, but it was a distant memory. And she knew for certain Richard never had.

She shook it off and started counting her paces, and in her hurry she couldn't remember if she did the thirties, so she counted them again. The consistency of the ground beneath her changed. Her feet slipped on loose rock, and then it was something entirely different. Entirely flat. And entirely hard.

She heard the creak and give of whatever was beneath her moments before there was a sharp *snap* and it all gave way as she plummeted into nothingness. She screamed. She couldn't help it.

Her hands grasped for purchase, slowing her down as she went into the mine shaft. Her hip slammed against a metal railing just before she hit the bottom with an *oomph*, knocking the air out of her.

"Wow, this sucks," she said, panting. "Look on the bright side. This is probably a good hiding place."

Chapter Six

Grant put Liza and her safety out of his mind. It was time to go hunting.

He snugged the submachine gun against his chest and moved quickly between areas of cover, stopping to listen. Sound was deceptive out here, where echoes made things seem closer than they really were. He could've sworn he heard the rev of a motorcycle engine, which would have been Caine's preferred method of transportation. She loved hitting the open road on her bike.

His eyes had adjusted to the dark, but the terrain of Montana was nothing like the streets of Detroit. He was an urban warrior. All cop and not a mountain man. He'd not had the benefit of extensive land navigation training in the military like many of his task force counterparts. His jungle was constructed of concrete and steel and glass. None of which did him any good in this environment.

Grant knelt to make himself as small a target as possible to escape some of the peppering effects of the wind's gusts. He concentrated on his breathing to slow his heartbeat and try to single out where Caine was. Eyes and ears and gut instinct. It was all he had.

Then he saw it—the small orb bouncing across the craggy

ground. Her motorcycle would be upon him in a matter of minutes. He leveled his submachine gun across the horizon. He'd wait until she drew closer and lay down a line of fire. It wasn't a sure hit, but it might be enough to knock her off or destroy her transportation.

Grant took several deep breaths and then held the last one, so his body lay completely still. The earth was cold beneath him and it felt like he was lying on frozen peas, but his concentration was absolute.

He blinked the grit from his watering eyes. His right index finger applied pressure to the trigger. All it would take was seven pounds of pull on the trigger and his compact rifle would unleash hell fire on the approaching assassin. He steadied his sight along the barrel. He saw the headlamp jostling across the ground, and it didn't appear to slow up at all as it drew within about two hundred yards from him. She didn't know where he was, and the advantage was his.

An explosion of sizzling red and orange rocketed into the sky from somewhere to his right, and he immediately let out a string of curses as he realized Liza had shot off one of the flares. The motorcycle skidded to a halt, the engine still running, and he swore he could hear Caine's laughter. The game was still on.

She was so close, if he moved she would've been alerted to his presence, and Grant was caught between cursing Liza and wondering if she was okay. Shooting the flare was like giving Caine a damned map to her location. Before he could reposition his sights, Caine turned the motorcycle in the opposite direction and took off with a spew of rocks and dirt toward the mountains. Toward the area they were traveling to get to Thomas's cabin.

He waited a few minutes until he could no longer see or hear her, and then he scrambled to his feet and started running in the direction the flare had come from.

"Liza," Grant said, once he thought he was in the general area.

"Grant?" she asked, her voice shaky and muffled.

Fear gripped him. He never should've let her go out on her own. She wasn't equipped with survival skills. She baked naughty cakes for a living. What had he been thinking?

"Liza," he said again. "Tell me where you are, honey."

Her voice was a little louder this time when she answered. "I fell in a hole. Be careful."

He'd already noticed the disruption along the ground. The broken timbers and scattered rocks and leaves that must have been covering it. She was lucky she hadn't broken her neck. The weight of guilt pressed down on him.

"Are you hurt?" he asked.

"I sprained my ankle, but nothing is broken. Sorry about the flare, but I didn't know what else to do."

"It's okay," he said. "Let's get you out of there while we can. I think we have a little breathing room. Caine took off north."

"Where we're headed?" she asked, the defeat clear in her voice.

"It's all right. I've got a plan. We just need to get you out of there and walking."

Grant shined the mounted high-powered light from the barrel of his weapon into the shaft's opening.

"I don't suppose you noticed…"

"The ladder?" she asked, interrupting him. "Yes, I did notice. I also noticed I have a sprained ankle and that it looks about as safe as a turkey at Thanksgiving."

Grant's mouth quirked. Damned if he didn't like her sassy mouth. "Are you able to walk at all?"

"Yeah, I can walk. It just hurts like a bitch."

He went to the ladder, and though it did look like it had seen better days, it seemed to be sturdy enough to get Liza out. She hobbled over to the ladder and he caught a good glimpse of her in his light. His smile widened. Her tight jeans were ripped at the knees and she was covered in mud. There were spider webs in her hair, though he had a gut feeling that was something he probably shouldn't tell her. If he thought she'd looked like Xena Warrior

Princess when he'd first seen her, she *really* looked like her now.

He'd never felt such instant attraction to another person. He was by nature a loner, and it took him a while to make friends, and even longer to trust them. And he'd never put much stock in his relationships because his career had always come first. But he was drawn to Liza, and there was something refreshingly honest about her. She wasn't the type to play games, and she said exactly what she thought.

He put his rifle down and lay on his belly, and then he reached down to help pull her up so she didn't have to put so much weight on her ankle. When she came out of the hole, she lay on her back a few minutes, breathing in the night air and calming herself.

"I'm not a fan of small, dark places," she said. "And I'm really not a fan of spiders."

He pressed his lips together and brushed her hair back nonchalantly, as if he were stroking her instead of removing the spider webs.

"You did good, Xena." And before he knew what he was doing, he leaned down and kissed her—softly—tenderly—and he knew he'd be in deep trouble with this woman if he let himself.

"Thanks, Hercules," she said. She seemed surprised by the kiss. As surprised as he was. But she smiled cheekily and tried to make light of things. "What's your big plan?"

"To go back to Surrender," he told her. "She thinks she knows what we're going to do next, but Caine's downfall is that she's always been impatient. The longer we don't engage in her game of cat and mouse, the more irritated she'll become. Then the tide will turn and she'll come looking for us. It's time to let her find us."

"Well," Liza said, blowing out a breath and coming gingerly to her feet. "That sounds crazy as hell. Let's do it."

"Don't be mad at me for suggesting this," he said, "but with the shape that ankle is in, you might be better off back in the hole and letting me get in touch with Deputy Greyson or one of the

MacKenzies to come get you."

"Honey, I'm Canadian. We're tougher than we look." Liza slapped him on the ass, causing his mouth to drop open, and then she started walking, her gait slowed by the limp.

He had to give it to her. She was a hell of a woman.

"Aren't you coming?" she called back over her shoulder.

"Yep," he said, "but you're going the wrong direction."

Chapter Seven

Liza was starting to doubt her Canadian toughness by the time downtown Surrender came back into view. They'd heard the echo of the motorcycle in the distance, but there'd been no headlight to show them Caine's position like before, so they'd picked up the pace. When she'd stumbled for the fourth time, Grant had shifted his weapon to his right side and put his arm around her to help support her weight.

She was bone tired, her body hurt, and she would've killed for some water and something to eat. But Grant was steady beside her, and it made her feel safer and more secure. Downtown was as quiet and desolate as it had been when they'd left. Even the sheriff's office was still locked up tight.

She'd learned during her time in Surrender that the people there lived a different kind of life. A life where family always came first and the people were friendly. Where businesses were planted with the ideal of the American dream and not a way to get rich quick, and where farmers and ranchers were still appreciated and regarded for the things they provided and their hard work ethic. She'd never seen anything like it in her life, and though it was easy to mock the early bedtimes and the lack of nightlife, it wasn't easy to come to terms with the fact that maybe it was *she* that needed to change and accept instead of the town. Because she was coming to find that living in Surrender was…nice.

The sheriff's office was just as empty as when they'd left, but that wasn't surprising. She hoped Lane Greyson was snuggled in bed next to his wife, Naya. Talk about a woman who looked like she didn't belong in Surrender. But somehow she made it work. Made herself fit. And the people there accepted her for who she was.

"You really think she'll come back here?" she asked, panting as she tried to catch her breath.

They were crouched between cars in the parking lot, eyeing the door of the upstairs apartment. They were so close, but it seemed as far away as the thought of going that initial ten miles had. She wasn't sure she could make it any farther.

"Yeah," he said. "I really think she'll come back here."

"Grant, I've got to tell you something," she said.

"I hope it's not that you've got to go to the bathroom, because this really isn't a good time."

She snickered before she could help it and slapped him on the arm. She was delirious.

"I was going to tell you that I'm glad I met you. Despite all this stuff. This has made me realize some things about myself that I didn't know before. So I thank you for that."

He squeezed her hand and said, "I'm just sorry I dragged you into this mess. And I'm sorry your bakery got damaged. I know you've got plans."

"I've never been too big a believer in plans," she said, shrugging. "Plans have a tendency to change."

"That they do, Xena. That they do."

They scooted between the parked cars until they were at the very edge, and they had a full view of the back of the sheriff's office and the stairs that led up to the second story apartment.

"We've still got to make it up those stairs," he said. "That's going to be the hard part. When we're most exposed."

"And I'm going to slow us down," she said, biting her lip.

"Let's just focus on getting up there. It'll be daylight soon. I can't see her continuing this once folks return to town to open their shops," Grant said. "If we're lucky a task force will be in place sometime tomorrow, but if we can end this now the more lives later on that are likely to be saved. Stay low and head straight for the stairs. Got it?"

"I've got it," she said.

And then they took off. She forgot about the pain shooting up her ankle or that she was tired. Her adrenaline was kicking so high she was moving faster than she'd expected, and her only focus was that staircase. She trusted Grant to keep them safe.

She stopped in her tracks at the unmistakable sound of gunfire. The first bullet bounced off the handrail just feet in front of them, splintering the wood. Liza felt the sting above her left wrist and looked down to see blood pooling from the sliver of wood that had cut her.

"Don't stop," Grant yelled.

But that was easier said than done. In her shock and panic, she froze. And then she looked back in time to see the shadow of the figure who'd been hunting them. Until the shadow turned into flesh and blood and they stood face to face with Ryan Caine.

Liza would've laughed if she hadn't been scared shitless. Ryan Caine looked like the stereotypical James Bond assassin. Against the dim light that hung outside of the sheriff's office, she saw a tall, built woman with close-cropped auburn hair. The cuteness of her pixie cut contrasted with her cold-hearted killer lifestyle, but she seemed very comfortable with the weapon in her hand. The weapon still pointed at them. A second shot tore into the wall beside her and she tumbled into Grant's arms.

"Get down," he said, practically shoving her toward an old Tahoe with the sheriff's logo emblazoned on the side. Grant came in right behind her and she scooted out of his way, curling into a ball. He let off a volley of shots as they covered down, then he grabbed Liza's wrist to stem the blood, but she pulled his hand away.

"It's just a scratch," she exhaled.

"Damn it, that was way too close," Grant said. His breath came out in white puffs and the hard gleam in his eyes gave her pause. This was Grant the warrior. Not the lover or smartass. And that cold, blank stare scared the hell out of her.

"Don't take this the wrong way, but she's fucking crazy," Liza said. "Gorgeous. But crazy."

"That pretty much sums it up," he said.

Grant ducked and covered Liza's head with his body as three or four more shots shattered the windows of the Tahoe.

Liza saw the panic on Grant's face as something that sounded like a metal clink and then what sounded like a soft drink can hit the ground.

"Oh, shit," he said, and then pressed his hand over her eyes.

An incredible eruption of noise deafened her, and although Grant's hand covered her face, she still saw the blinding white light through his hand. Speckles of light burst behind her eyelids and she saw the blood vessels running within them. Her heart thudded in her chest, as if someone had turned the bass up too loud, and her body throbbed from the blast of the concussion.

"Flash-bang," she thought she heard Grant say, but she wasn't sure.

She shook her head once and still little flashes of lights danced in front of her eyes. "What was that?" she asked.

"She tossed a flash-bang. It's meant to disorient."

"It worked," she said.

"She's playing more games. It's time to play back. I need to get you up the stairs. There are more weapons up there." He handed her the keys to unlock the upstairs door. "Barricade yourself inside."

"And?" Liza's eyes popped wide.

"You ever shot a gun before?" he asked.

"I'm from Canada," she said. "What do you think?"

He sighed and said, "Right. You point and pull the trigger."

"I can't shoot anyone," she said, panicking.

"Just shoot at the ground. It'll distract her enough that maybe

I can get a money shot in."

"Just so you know, in the naughty-cake-baking world, a money shot is something totally different."

He burst out laughing and reloaded his weapon. "You're a hell of a woman, Liza Carmichael."

"You're not so bad yourself."

"I'm going to reach into this cruiser and activate the top lights. The flashing strobes will blind her for a moment, but she'll think it's a distraction. I'll start popping rounds her way to keep her head down."

Liza leaned up and kissed him. "Say when."

Grant eased the car door open, and it creaked like a rusted screen door hinge. The interior light beamed over him, and she bit her lip as his fingers crawled across the cloth seat and over to the control panel in the center console, flipping on the switches.

Suddenly, a disco of flashing strobe lights whipped around the parking lot. He'd also activated the alley lights, and the high-beam lights were super powerful. Grant popped up and began shooting toward the direction he'd last seen Caine.

"Move," he yelled over the gunfire.

She moved. She ran for everything she was worth toward the stairs, the blood rushing so loudly in her ears she could barely hear the gunfire. She reached the top and was amazed it only took her three tries to get the key in the door and get it unlocked.

She shoved open the door and fell to the floor, kicking it closed behind her. Her heart raced and her ears buzzed. She heard the commotion continue below.

"Shit," she said. "Gotta lay down fire."

She went to the dining room table where Grant had set out his collection of weapons and she picked up the pistol. "Point and pull the trigger," she reminded herself of his instructions. "Just shoot into the ground. I can do that."

She went to the window and pulled up the blinds, and she heard another volley of gunfire. A bullet hit the window and she'd never in her life been so glad for bulletproof glass. That thought made her a little more brave and she peeked through to the scene down below. She could see Grant still crouched behind the Tahoe and Caine not far away, using another vehicle for a shield.

The gunfire continued and she knew she had to do her part, so she sucked in a deep breath and opened the window, staying to the side in case Caine shot in her direction again.

"You can do this, Liza. Just stay low and shoot at the ground."

Just as she got into position and was ready to pull the trigger, the firing stopped. There was nothing. Not even the sound of weapons being reloaded.

She heard glass breaking below and fear overtook her. Looking out the window showed her nothing. There was no sign of Caine. No sign of Grant. For all she knew he could be lying dead in a puddle of his own blood.

Then she heard the creak from the trapdoor of the passage that led to the sheriff's office below, and the slam as the door closed again.

"Grant," she called out, hating the fact that her voice shook.

But it wasn't Grant, and she thought her worst fear might have come true. Grant was dead and now she was left to face this insane woman. This was not how she'd expected to die.

"You fat bitch," Caine said. "Did you really think you'd get away from me? Grant likes to put his women in danger. I think he has psychological issues, so I wouldn't get too invested." Caine smiled, and she was even more beautiful, but the insanity darkened it.

Rage like nothing she'd ever known swept through Liza's body, and she was hot all over. Other than driving her car into Richard's house, she wouldn't have considered herself a violent person. But she was feeling pretty violent at the moment.

"Who are you calling fat?" she yelled back.

Liza gripped the pistol and pointed it at Caine. The thick, rubberized custom-grip felt heavy yet conformed within her palm. She eased her finger through the trigger guard's opening and settled it against the ridged curve of the short trigger.

She pulled the trigger and a bullet pinged far to Caine's right. Ceramics and a plate exploded off the bookshelf in the living room. Liza's ears rang, and she hadn't been expecting the kick from the gun. Her wrist was throbbing.

Caine leapt back and away, but Liza didn't stop. She continued to track her and ripped off another bullet, this one closer to the mark. They were doing a dance, Caine moving clockwise and Liza following her.

She pressed her lips tight and squeezed the trigger again, this time into the pots and a black skillet that hung over the stove.

"Fuck," she yelled. They didn't make it look so hard in the movies.

She shot again, and this time the bullet embedded itself into the wall just a couple of feet from her nemesis. Liza's eyes narrowed and she focused. This time when she pulled the trigger the bullet bounced against the top of the bulletproof window. The same window she'd opened earlier.

Caine leapt through the open window and was gone just as Liza pulled the trigger one last time. But there was nothing but an empty click. She was out of bullets.

"That'll show you who's fat," she said.

Chapter Eight

"Open this damn door or I'll blast through it," Grant yelled.

Liza stood frozen, the hot barrel smoldering in her hand. "Holy shit," she said. "I'm like Annie Oakley."

"Liza," Grant said, pounding his fist against the door.

"Sorry," she called out. "Coming."

She unlocked the deadbolt and Grant pushed through the door before she could open it for him. He pulled her into his arms and pressed his cheek against the top of her.

"Jesus, woman. You scared the hell out of me."

"How'd she get past you?" she said, her body starting to shake uncontrollably.

"She threw another flash-bang and laid down fire as she ran. Cooper's going to be pissed. She shot through the windows downstairs. I'm not sure how she knew about the trapdoor that leads up here, but more than likely she was probably listening to us with a Bionic Ear or some kind of technology. It's not hard to come by."

Liza gripped him harder. "Do you think she was listening to…everything?"

"It's probably best not to think about it." He took the gun

from her shaking hand and checked the magazine. "I don't suppose you hit her?"

She narrowed her eyes at him. "No, but I probably scared the hell out of her. I would've been better off throwing the damned thing at her. I'm sorry I let her get away."

"Don't be sorry. We'll get her. Let's get you off that foot and take a look at it."

Her body shook uncontrollably and her teeth were chattering. If she'd closed her eyes in that moment, she thought she might have fallen asleep standing up. He helped her get settled in one of the chairs, and then he leaned in slowly to kiss her. It was so simple—just a kiss—and then his forehead rested against hers for a second. He went into the kitchen and grabbed a bag of ice before heading into the bathroom for the first-aid kit.

They were both in need of patching up. Grant's face was still covered in blood and it looked like he had some fresh wounds. She didn't want to even think about what she looked like. Definitely *not* G.I. Jane material though.

"You think she's coming back?" she asked when he came back in with the supplies.

"I think she's close. But I don't think she'll come back up here. I closed the window, by the way. We're secure for the moment. It's more likely she'll try to burn us out."

"Lovely," she said, but she couldn't muster up the strength to be more scared.

He'd washed his face, but there were still cuts oozing blood. He didn't seem to notice. But he handed her a medicated towelette to clean off the cut at her wrist, and then he knelt at her feet.

"This is probably going to hurt like hell when I take your shoe off. It's been keeping your ankle compressed. More than likely the swelling is going to go up."

"I don't think it's too bad," she said, her hands turning to fists as he unknotted her laces and pulled very carefully at the shoe. "The more I walked on it the more it loosened up."

By the time he got both her sock and shoe off, she was shaking again and her cheeks were wet with tears.

"Oh, baby. Don't cry. I know it hurts. I'm so sorry." His words were soothing and gentle, but she couldn't seem to stop the tears.

"I'm not crying because of that," she said, sniffling loudly. Her foot wasn't too terrible. It was discolored and a little swollen, and it'd probably keep her from wearing her favorite boots for a while, but she could live with it.

"Why are you crying?" he asked as he started wrapping her foot in an ACE bandage, and then he stopped halfway and laid the bag of ice over the swollen area before he finished wrapping it.

"I…I don't know…why I'm crying," she said, crying even harder. "I can't help it." Sobs wracked her body, and if she could've crawled into the nearest hole, she would've gone there gladly. She was mortified. "And now I'm crying because I'm embarrassed because I never cry. Do you think I'm crazy?"

"No, I think you're normal," he said. "Though I did think you were a little crazy when you told me you drove through a man's house, but I've reevaluated now that I've gotten to know you better."

She sniffed and laughed. "Good to know. I think that day was a culmination of years of pent up anger coming to the surface. Very un-Canadian of me."

"If it makes you feel better, you seem to be adapting to the American way of life pretty well. And what's happening to you now is perfectly normal. I've seen the most hardened cop break down a hell of a lot worse than you just did. It's all part of the experience. It's just your body's way of coping with the trauma."

He wrapped her in a soft blanket and then leaned in to kiss her again. "You did good, Carmichael."

Liza had never let herself get close to a man emotionally. She'd always had that fear that letting herself get in too deep would lead to disaster, like it had with her parents. She hadn't really even loved Richard, and she certainly hadn't had the connection with him where she felt comfortable bearing her soul. She'd always held part of herself in reserve.

But she could feel that part of herself she'd walled off start to break down with Grant. Maybe because she hadn't had a choice. The high-stakes circumstances had changed the game and made her reevaluate some things about her life. And the physical connection had only amplified the emotional connection. She was confused.

Once they were bandaged and wrapped, Grant found a couple of bottles of water. She drank it down greedily. Grant went to check the back windows.

"There's no sign of her in the parking lot," he said.

He moved to the front window that overlooked Main Street. "I talked to Lane Greyson while I was in the bathroom getting supplies. He and a few others are putting the town on lockdown, going door-to-door and making phone calls. Hopefully we can spare innocent people from walking into this mess. I talked to Cooper again too, now that he's not loopy with drugs, and he's been in contact with MacKenzie Security. All of the field agents are gone on a big assignment at the moment, so we're kind of shit out of luck there.

"Coop said he's calling in favors, and they're working on putting a task force together. But that takes time in this area, and Caine knows that. It's mostly you and me, kid, until the cavalry arrives. The other deputies have their hands full making sure everyone else stays safe. She'll strike before daylight and then get the hell out of town. If she doesn't want someone to find her, they won't."

"You've got a plan?" she asked.

He smiled and said, "I'm going to scale out of the building through the roof. I'll get your BMW and pick you up. We need to try and get to the MacKenzie compound. We'll be safe there."

He reloaded her weapon and handed it back to her. Liza shook her head, feeling the panic claw inside of her. "I can't," she said. "I'm not Annie Oakley."

"You don't have to be. All you have to do is make sure you protect yourself, and unloading a magazine full of ammunition at someone will accomplish that task."

"Right," she muttered. "Just scare the hell out of her."

"That's the spirit," he said. He handed her her purse, and she dug for the key fob to give to him. He turned to leave, but she grabbed his arm to pull him back.

"Kiss me good-bye," she said, the desperation in her voice unmistakable. She wasn't stupid. She knew there was a chance Grant might not make it back to her.

"It's not good-bye," he said. "I'm just going to get the car. I'll be back before you know it."

"A kiss," she demanded. And then she hoisted herself up from the chair and hobbled toward him. He met her halfway, and she leaned forward to whisper in his ear. "And when you come back alive and we're not being hunted by a maniac, I'm going to strip you naked and ride you until you can't see straight."

He groaned and his fingers bit into her hips. She immediately felt the hardness of his cock against her stomach. Even with everything they'd been through that night, she wondered if there was time to feel him inside her one more time. The thought it might never happen again terrified her.

Almost as if he'd read her mind, he kissed her hard, his tongue delving deep into her mouth.

"I'll be back," he said. "Count on it. Listen for the beep of the car when it unlocks. Once you hear it, head downstairs and be ready to roll."

* * * *

Grant pulled down the attic access panel stairs and climbed up. All of the shops on Main Street had roof access through the attic for safety reasons. He found the square window that led up to the roof and unlatched it, giving it a little extra shove since it had been a while since it had been used.

The rush of cold air slapped his cheeks and dried out his eyes. If it hadn't been dark, he would've been a sitting duck up there, waiting to be picked off. He lifted himself up and rolled so he lay flat on the roof. There was no sound, no explosion of gunfire. He belly crawled across the flat roof before dropping down onto the roof of Captured Moments Photography studio.

Grant lay still and let his eyes and breathing adjust. The street awnings made it impossible to see if Caine was directly below him—he'd need a ladder down the backside of the row of buildings. He slithered across the studio's roof and peeked over the backside. *Nothing.* He'd have to get over to the Mercantile building.

The roof of the Mercantile was a half-level higher than Captured Moments, so he shoved his pistol into his jeans to climb the wall. He hated not having his gun immediately available. He sensed Caine's presence, but he had to keep moving. Liza's BMW wasn't far away. They might even take a few bullets as they made their escape, but he knew there was no chance of survival if they stayed in Cooper's place.

His hands ached and the sharp edge of the Mercantile roof cut into his stomach as he hefted himself up and dragged himself over the edge. Grant grunted as he kicked his right leg up. He hooked his heel onto the flashing. It took everything he had left to hoist his body onto the elevated pitch. There was a break in the awning. All he had to do was get down and get across the street. That was when he'd be most vulnerable.

Grant squatted at the ledge's edge, letting the wind slap him in the face. He was exhausted, but there was still work to be done. He'd been through hell and back, but between Caine's deadly cat-and-mouse game, and Liza's tempting him with every thought, Grant looked forward to putting this nightmare behind him.

He climbed down until he hung from the edge, and then dropped the rest of the way to the ground, staying crouched low and on the balls of his feet in case he needed to move quickly. He looked to his left and to his right. Both seemed clear. He yanked the 9mm out of his jeans and then fished the key fob from his pocket.

Almost there.

And then he felt the barrel of a weapon press into the back of his skull.

"Tag, you're dead," Caine said.

Chapter Nine

"He's taking too long," Liza said to herself. The window was open just a crack, enough that she could hear, but there'd been nothing but silence. "Come on, Grant."

In all honesty, she wasn't great at waiting. Waiting made her a nervous wreck. And the thought of Caine out there with Grant was driving her crazy. Caine could only watch one of them at a time, and Grant was by far the bigger threat. If he was in trouble, she'd be damned if she just sat there and waited for Caine to come pick her off.

She dug in her purse for the spare key fob, and she shoved the pistol into the pocket of her sweatshirt. Or whoever's sweatshirt she was wearing. Getting down the ladder was going to be the tricky part. Her foot was aching, and since she'd been off it for a bit it was starting to stiffen up.

She'd been listening for the double beep that the car made when it was unlocked, but so far she'd heard a big fat lot of nothing. And she hadn't seen him cross the street to the bakery side, where she'd parked the car. Liza knew that would be when he was most vulnerable, and maybe he was just biding his time, but her gut was telling her it was something else entirely. He'd had plenty of time to get down to ground level and make a break for it across the street.

She opened the trapdoor that led downstairs and tried to hold back a whimper as she put pressure on her ankle.

"Be tough, be tough," she whispered over and over again.

She felt the draft immediately at the back of the sheriff's office, where Caine had opened fire on the cargo door and windows. Grant was right. Cooper was going to be pissed at the damage done.

Since the hole was already made, she went out the back, taking the pistol from her sweatshirt and keeping it pointed at the ground. Her teeth chattered as she made her way around the side of the building until she stood at the outside corner of the sheriff's office, directly facing the bakery.

There was no sign of Grant, and she eased around the corner, looking both directions up and down the street. There wasn't a soul. And part of her wondered if maybe he found another way of escape and had decided to leave her behind.

"No, he wouldn't do that," she assured herself. Grant had a strict moral code. She'd known him less than twenty-four hours and already she knew that about him.

The bitter bite of the March winds whipped hair across her face. She could see the shiny red Beemer from where she stood, still parked illegally at the side of the bakery. Thank goodness she'd parked out of range from the corner windows. No one would be able to see her get into the car unless they were standing with their face pressed against the glass and looking toward the parking lot.

She was just about to take a leap of faith and head to the other side of the street when she heard the muffled sound of voices and jumped back so she was protected by the wall of the sheriff's office.

"Keep moving," Caine said.

Liza knelt down and tried to make herself invisible as she watched Grant being marched across the street, a gun to the back of his head. He looked entirely too calm for her peace of mind. Which meant he was probably going to play the hero and get himself killed in the process.

"Stubborn man," she hissed, and then her own plan formed in her mind and she scooted around to the back side of the businesses along Main Street.

The good thing about the street was that it was barely a block long. She hobbled past the photography studio, the Mercantile, the ice cream parlor, the bookstore, and the florist before she got to the opposite end of where she'd been. Caine and Grant were already inside the bakery, and she knew every second was precious, so she sucked in a deep breath and ran as fast as her ankle would allow across the cobbled street.

Then she hobbled her way behind the buildings on the other side of the street until she saw the Beemer sitting there in the lot. She moved closer and chewed on her bottom lip, her finger hovering over the unlock button.

"To hell with it," she said and ran to the driver's side door, hitting the remote start as she went.

She waited until the quiet engine purred to life and then put her hand on the handle, the doors automatically unlocking. If she was lucky, Caine wouldn't have heard a thing. If she was unlucky…well…it was best not to think of that.

The leather seat molded around her aching body, and she cut the headlights off. Then she threw the car in reverse and headed back the exact way she'd come, only she pulled behind and to the far side of the library because there wasn't a direct shot from the bakery to where she was sitting.

The front light was on in the bakery and she could see the two of them in there through the corner window. The front windows had been boarded up by some kind soul. It didn't look like Grant had much to say. Caine was doing all the talking and she looked to be getting more irritated by the second.

The sky had turned a pearl gray at some point, but Liza could still see them clearly. What she didn't know was if Caine would be able to see her once the sun was fully out.

Grant just stood there, his body rigid, as Caine paced circles around him, taunting him like an animal in a cage.

Why didn't he try to fight? Try to run? Then she watched in horror as Caine raised the barrel of her rifle, and she slapped a hand over her mouth to keep from screaming.

And then something took over inside of her—gone was the fear of facing down an enemy. Her only thought was that she couldn't let Grant die. Her hands tightened around the steering wheel, and her knuckles went white. She knew it was now or never. Caine had the rifle holding steady on Grant and she'd stopped talking.

"You bitch," Liza yelled and slammed her foot on the gas pedal.

The BMW shot forward and accelerated quickly. She didn't give a thought to the fact that the building had been in her family for generations, or the fact that she was going to have a hell of a time selling pastries with a gaping hole in the front. All she cared about was Grant.

The car gained speed as she covered the short distance within seconds. She went straight at the corner window, bracing herself for the impact. The wheels hopped the wooden sidewalk first before crashing straight through the bakery. Caine turned and Grant took advantage of the distraction to dive out of the way.

Caine didn't have time to point the rifle in her direction and pull the trigger before the front end of the car took her down. The airbags exploded and Liza's seatbelt tightened as she was jerked forward.

Bile rose in her throat at the thought that she'd just run over a human being. She reminded herself Grant would be dead if she hadn't, and then she tried to take a couple of steadying breaths.

Then the car door jerked open and she stifled a scream, thinking she might not have run over Caine good enough.

"Holy shit, woman," he said, unfastening her seatbelt since she couldn't seem to move. "Don't you ever scare me again like that."

Liza felt like she was having an out-of-body experience. She couldn't form a coherent thought, much less a sentence, and all she could seem to do was whimper as he gathered her in his arms.

"Oh, baby," he said. "You're bleeding."

She tried to open her mouth to speak, but nothing came out.

"You came for me," he said, kissing her gently on the forehead. "That was very brave of you. Incredibly stupid, but very brave."

"S…sorry," she managed to get out through chattering teeth.

"Don't look," he said when she tried to turn her head. "She's dead. I made sure. You did what you had to do. I'm not saying you won't have guilt or hurt or even nightmares, but you saved my life, and I can never repay you for that."

"You can start by getting me out of here and finding us a bed to sleep in for a full eight hours. I think I'm about to pass out."

"Done," he said. "I can't believe you drove through your building. What the hell are you going to be able to do with it now?"

She burrowed in close and breathed in his scent. "I'm going to do a hell of a remodel and sell naughty cakes out of the back room. What do you think of that?"

"That you're going to turn this town on its ear and everyone is going to love it. I've been thinking maybe I should take Cooper up on that deputy job. He's going to be out a while and he's going to need help getting things back in order. Besides, after the last twenty-four hours, I'm ready for the slow life."

"What's that?"

"Getting up, going to work, flirting with a beautiful woman over naughty pastries, and then doing naughty things to her behind the counter."

"Hmm," she said. "Sounds promising."

"There's only one problem," he said, and she felt her heart clutch in her chest.

"What's that?"

"This place is going to need a new name to go with its new owner."

She smiled. "That's easy, baby. I'm calling it Sweet Surrender."

* * * *

Also from 1001 Dark Nights and Liliana Hart, discover Captured in Surrender, Trouble Maker, and The Promise of Surrender.

Sign up for the 1001 Dark Nights Newsletter
and be entered to win a Tiffany Key necklace.

There's a contest every month!

Go to www.1001DarkNights.com to subscribe.

As a bonus, all subscribers will receive a free
1001 Dark Nights story
The First Night
by Lexi Blake & M.J. Rose

Turn the page for a full list of the
1001 Dark Nights fabulous novellas...

Discover 1001 Dark Nights Collection Three

HIDDEN INK by Carrie Ann Ryan
A Montgomery Ink Novella

BLOOD ON THE BAYOU by Heather Graham
A Cafferty & Quinn Novella

SEARCHING FOR MINE by Jennifer Probst
A Searching For Novella

DANCE OF DESIRE by Christopher Rice

ROUGH RHYTHM by Tessa Bailey
A Made In Jersey Novella

DEVOTED by Lexi Blake
A Masters and Mercenaries Novella

Z by Larissa Ione
A Demonica Underworld Novella

FALLING UNDER YOU by Laurelin Paige
A Fixed Trilogy Novella

EASY FOR KEEPS by Kristen Proby
A Boudreaux Novella

UNCHAINED by Elisabeth Naughton
An Eternal Guardians Novella

HARD TO SERVE by Laura Kaye
A Hard Ink Novella

DRAGON FEVER by Donna Grant
A Dark Kings Novella

KAYDEN/SIMON by Alexandra Ivy/Laura Wright
A Bayou Heat Novella

STRUNG UP by Lorelei James
A Blacktop Cowboys® Novella

MIDNIGHT UNTAMED by Lara Adrian
A Midnight Breed Novella

TRICKED by Rebecca Zanetti
A Dark Protectors Novella

DIRTY WICKED by Shayla Black
A Wicked Lovers Novella

THE ONLY ONE by Lauren Blakely
A One Love Novella

SWEET SURRENDER by Liliana Hart
A MacKenzie Family Novella

For more information, go to www.1001DarkNights.com.

Discover 1001 Dark Nights Collection One

FOREVER WICKED by Shayla Black
CRIMSON TWILIGHT by Heather Graham
CAPTURED IN SURRENDER by Liliana Hart
SILENT BITE: A SCANGUARDS WEDDING by Tina Folsom
DUNGEON GAMES by Lexi Blake
AZAGOTH by Larissa Ione
NEED YOU NOW by Lisa Renee Jones
SHOW ME, BABY by Cherise Sinclair
ROPED IN by Lorelei James
TEMPTED BY MIDNIGHT by Lara Adrian
THE FLAME by Christopher Rice
CARESS OF DARKNESS by Julie Kenner

Also from 1001 Dark Nights

TAME ME by J. Kenner

For more information, go to www.1001DarkNights.com.

Discover 1001 Dark Nights Collection Two

WICKED WOLF by Carrie Ann Ryan
WHEN IRISH EYES ARE HAUNTING by Heather Graham
EASY WITH YOU by Kristen Proby
MASTER OF FREEDOM by Cherise Sinclair
CARESS OF PLEASURE by Julie Kenner
ADORED by Lexi Blake
HADES by Larissa Ione
RAVAGED by Elisabeth Naughton
DREAM OF YOU by Jennifer L. Armentrout
STRIPPED DOWN by Lorelei James
RAGE/KILLIAN by Alexandra Ivy/Laura Wright
DRAGON KING by Donna Grant
PURE WICKED by Shayla Black
HARD AS STEEL by Laura Kaye
STROKE OF MIDNIGHT by Lara Adrian
ALL HALLOWS EVE by Heather Graham
KISS THE FLAME by Christopher Rice
DARING HER LOVE by Melissa Foster
TEASED by Rebecca Zanetti
THE PROMISE OF SURRENDER by Liliana Hart

Also from 1001 Dark Nights

THE SURRENDER GATE By Christopher Rice
SERVICING THE TARGET By Cherise Sinclair

For more information, go to www.1001DarkNights.com.

About Liliana Hart

Liliana Hart is a *New York Times*, *USA Today*, and Publisher's Weekly Bestselling Author of more than 50 titles. After starting her first novel her freshman year of college, she immediately became addicted to writing and knew she'd found what she was meant to do with her life. She has no idea why she majored in music.

Since self-publishing in June of 2011, Liliana has sold more than 5 million ebooks and been translated into eight languages. She's appeared at #1 on lists all over the world and all three of her series have appeared on the *New York Times* list. Liliana is a sought after speaker and she's given keynote speeches and self-publishing workshops to standing-room-only crowds from California to New York to London.

Liliana can almost always be found at her computer writing or on the road giving workshops for SilverHart International, a company she founded with her husband, Scott Silverii, where they provide law enforcement, military, and fire resources for writers so they can write it right.

Connect with me online:
twitter.com/Liliana_Hart
facebook.com/LilianaHart
My Website: www.lilianahart.com

Discover More Liliana Hart

Captured in Surrender
A MacKenzie Family Novella
By Liliana Hart

Bounty Hunter Naya Blade never thought she'd step foot in Surrender, Montana again. Especially since there was a warrant out for her arrest. But when her skip ends up in the normally peaceful town, she has no choice but to go after him to claim her reward. Even at the cost of running into the cop that makes her blood run hot and her sense of self-preservation run cold.

Deputy Lane Greyson wants to see Naya in handcuffs, but he'd much prefer them attached to his bed instead of in a cold jail cell. She drove him crazy once before and then drove right out of town, leaving havoc in her wake. He's determined to help her hunt down the bad guy so he can claim his own bounty—her.

The Promise of Surrender
A MacKenzie Family Novella
By Liliana Hart

Mia Russo spent ten years working undercover, entrenched in the dregs of society before handing in her shield. Opening her own pawn shop is a piece of cake in comparison. All she needs is the bad attitude she developed on the streets and the shotgun under her counter to keep law and order. Until the day Zeke McBride walks into her shop.

Zeke knows Mia has every right not to trust him. He was the one who chose the next op instead of her. And all he can hope is that somewhere under the snarl and cynicism is a woman who can forgive. Because whether she trusts him or not, they're going to have to work together to bring down the gang that's decided Mia is their next target.

Trouble Maker
A MacKenzie Family Novel
By Liliana Hart

Marnie Whitlock has never known what it's like to be normal. Her ability to see the future and people's innermost thoughts makes her an outcast—feared—loathed. Even by her own parents. And her father is determined to beat the curse out of her. Her only chance for survival is to escape Surrender.

Beckett Hamilton has loved Marnie since they were kids, but one horrible night destroyed any future he'd hoped for. Now Marnie was back in Surrender, and picking up where they left off is the only thing on his mind. He finds out quickly that some hearts take longer to heal, and not everyone that's broken can be fixed. But loving Marnie isn't an option—it's his destiny.

Discover the MacKenzie Family World

Dear Readers,

I'm thrilled to be able to introduce the MacKenzie Family World to you. I asked ten of my favorite authors to create their own characters and put them into the world you all know and love. These amazing authors revisited Surrender, Montana, and through their imagination you'll get to meet new characters, while reuniting with some of your favorites.

These stories are hot, hot, hot—exactly what you'd expect from a MacKenzie story—and it was pure pleasure for me to read each and every one of them and see my world through someone else's eyes. They definitely did the series justice, and I hope you discover ten new authors to put on your auto-buy list.

Make sure you pre-order *Spies and Stilettos,* the very last MacKenzie novel, featuring fan favorites Brady Scott and Elana Nayal.

So grab a glass of wine, pour a bubble bath, and prepare to Surrender.

Love Always,

Liliana Hart

Available now!

Trouble Maker by Liliana Hart
Rush by Robin Covington
Bullet Proof by Avery Flynn
Delta: Rescue by Cristin Harber
Deep Trouble by Kimberly Kincaid
Desire & Ice by Christopher Rice

Coming March 21, 2017!

Spies & Stilettos by Liliana Hart
Never Surrender by Kaylea Cross
Avenged by Jay Crownover
Hot Witness by Lynn Raye Harris
Wicked Hot by Gennita Low
Hollow Point by Lili St. Germain

The Darkest Corner

Gravediggers
By Liliana Hart
Coming May 23, 2017
Available for pre-order here.

New York Times and *USA TODAY* bestselling author Liliana Hart's first book in her suspenseful Gravediggers series, featuring an elite group of mysterious men who might be dead to the world, but are also tasked with saving it—and no one can ever know.

The Gravediggers aren't exactly what they seem. They're the most elite of the world's fighting forces—and all they have in common is that they've been betrayed by the countries they've died for. Because they are dead. To their country, their military, and their families.

Sometimes the dead do rise...

Deacon Tucker is a dead man walking. A former black ops agent, he was disavowed and stripped of all honor before being recruited as a Gravedigger. But his honor and good name no longer matter, because no one knows he's alive, and he'll never get the recognition he deserves. His mission is simple: save the world or die trying. And for God's sake, don't ever fall in love. That's a rule punishable by death. The kind of death a man can't be brought back from.

Tess Sherman is the only mortician in Last Stop, Texas. She has no idea how Deacon Tucker ended up in her funeral home, but she'll eat her hat if he's *only* a funeral home assistant. Deacon is dangerous, deadly, and gorgeous. And she knows her attraction to him can only end in heartache.

Deacon is on a mission to stop the most fatal terror attack the world has ever known—what's known as The Day of

Destiny—a terrorist's dream. But when he discovers Tess has skills he can use to stop them, he has to decide if he can trust her with secrets worth dying for. And, most important, he has to decide if he can trust her with his heart.

* * * *

There was something about the time between three and four o'clock in the morning. When people with good intentions were tucked safely into their beds. When those without them crept into the alleyways like rats. And when warriors got shit done.

For Deacon Tucker, that meant it was time to get dirty.

The rain slapped against Deacon's face like tiny daggers. Lightning flashed—followed by sharp cracks of thunder—and the smell of ozone, wet dirt, and urgency lay heavy.

Deacon pushed his shovel deeper into the soggy ground, the muscles in his back straining as he lifted a mound of dirt and tossed it onto a pile over his shoulder. The four other members of his team did the same, each one stripped down to nothing but black cargo pants and combat boots, covered in a thick layer of mud. They worked in silence, an unspoken communication and familiarity between them.

The cemetery was old. It was a place where the oldest headstones told stories and the newer ones told a person's worth. It was where generations of those who shared blood now rested—a place for the elderly who had lived long and full lives and the young who had been taken too soon.

Heavy iron gates closed it off from the public after dark, and towering oaks had been planted in rows some hundred years earlier. Gnarled roots made the ground uneven, cracking the drive that snaked between the rows of headstones.

They worked by flashes of lightning and the sliver of moon that peeked around thunderheads. Everything was cast in shades of gray—from the pale marble of the headstones to the silver shimmer of water droplets as they collected on leaves and rained down on them. Black trunks speared menacingly from the ground—the branches creeping over them like bony arms.

The clank of metal on something solid made Deacon stop and look up at his brother in arms.

"I've got something," Axel said, letting his native Australian accent slip through. He pounded the tip of his shovel a couple of times against the top of the coffin.

Deacon nodded. "Let's get him uncovered. He's been here two days already. He doesn't have much longer. Grab the chains," he instructed Colin.

Deacon returned to the task at hand, doubling his efforts to clear the mud and water rapidly filling the hole. It was fortunate the casket was waterproof and had a rubberized seal around the lid. The rain had come steady for more than twenty-four hours, and changed their original timeline of removing Levi Wolffe from the ground the night before.

A man's life was at stake, and Wolffe had already been through more than most. It was going to be traumatic enough for him to wake up in a different country, surrounded by faces he'd never seen before, and unsure whether he'd been captured by the enemy. Fishing through the lies to get to the truth would take time.

Deacon knew *exactly* how Levi Wolffe was going to feel.

"Fuck me, this is a never-ending battle," Axel complained. "There's no way we're digging this thing all the way out of the muck."

"All we've got to do is uncover the handles on the sides," Deacon said. "We'll let the Bobcat do the rest."

"Got it, mate." Axel tossed his shovel out of the hole. "Give me a boost, will you?"

Deacon steepled his fingers together to make a sling and braced himself against the casket so he wouldn't slip. They were close to four feet down into the hole, but with the rain and mud, getting out wasn't going to be easy. Axel put his hand on Deacon's shoulder and his foot in the sling, and then grabbed for

Dante's hand as he was boosted up.

The casket was an upper end model—they had to be, for what they were used for—made of glossy oak and brass. Colin tossed Axel the chains, and he looped them through the handles on each side, using a carabiner to hold them together.

"Elias is ready to roll with the Bobcat," Axel called out, extending his arm to help Deacon out of the hole.

Deacon was two hundred and thirty pounds of solid muscle and a couple of inches over six feet. His boots and knees couldn't find purchase in the mud, and his grasp of Axel's hand was slipping. He finally grasped Axel's arm with both hands, hoisted his feet onto the coffin, and used his legs to push off, launching himself out of the grave.

Axel moved out of the way at the last second, and Deacon flew right into the pile of mud they'd dug up. He heard the snickers from Dante and Colin and took a fistful of mud in each hand as he got to his feet, launching it at them in quick succession. Elias's howls of laughter could be heard from inside the Bobcat.

"They'll both be out for vengeance now," Axel said, lips twitching in as close to a smile as he ever gave.

"I hope so," Deacon said. "I'd hate for things to get boring around the office."

The rain was coming down hard enough to rinse some of the mud from his torso, and he lifted his face to the sky to wash it from his cheeks. The thong tying his hair back had come loose and dark strands clung to his face. Thoughts of a hot shower and a beer were becoming a priority. Right after getting Levi Wolffe out of the ground.

"It was my understanding that Winter wasn't bringing any more of us in," Dante said as they hooked up the chains to the Bobcat and moved back out of the way. His accent was English, but he had the Italian genetics of his namesake. Dante was as refined and suave as any man Deacon had ever known. His clothes were always tailored, his haircuts expensive, and his knowledge of the finer things in life unparalleled. Standing in the pouring rain, covered in mud, was probably grating on him immensely.

"That's what she said, but who the hell knows what her plans are." Deacon had been wondering the same thing. "She only tells us what she thinks we need to know."

"Which isn't a bloody thing," Dante said.

It was a sore spot for certain. Deacon had served his country for most of his life. He'd been recruited by the CIA during his third year of college, the high scores on his aptitude tests and his skills for languages having alerted interested parties. His course in life had been clear from the moment that recruiter had left him. He'd gone on to get a master's degree and the necessary field training, which he'd also shown an exceptional aptitude for. In twelve years of covert ops, he'd never had a sleepless night after completing a mission. He'd gotten the job done. Until Eve Winter had gotten ahold of him, and everything he'd thought he'd been fighting for was turned on its head.

He didn't like being kept in the dark. He understood the hierarchy of a rank structure and the necessity of secrets. You couldn't survive in the CIA without that understanding. But his handler had once told him, "*Rules are for the obedience of fools and the guidance of wise men.*" Deacon had never been a fool.

On behalf of 1001 Dark Nights,
Liz Berry and M.J. Rose would like to thank ~

Steve Berry
Doug Scofield
Kim Guidroz
Jillian Stein
InkSlinger PR
Dan Slater
Asha Hossain
Chris Graham
Pamela Jamison
Fedora Chen
Jessica Johns
Dylan Stockton
Richard Blake
BookTrib After Dark
and Simon Lipskar

Printed in Great Britain
by Amazon